BILTMORE GIRL

BY
DAWN KLINGE

Dawn Klinge/Genevieve Publishing
dawn.klinge@gmail.com
www.dawnklingecom

Publisher's Note: This is a work of fiction. Names, characters, places, and incidents are a product of the author's imagination. Locales and public names are sometimes used for atmospheric purposes. Any resemblance to actual people, living or dead, or to businesses, companies, events, institutions, or locales is completely coincidental.

Book Layout ©2017 BookDesignTemplates.com

Cover design by Evelynne Labelle of Carpe Librum Book Design.

Biltmore Girl/ Dawn Klinge. -- 1st ed.
ISBN 978-1-7346434-2-8

Dedication

*To my son Trent. I believe God has a great
purpose for your life.*

""*For we are God's handiwork, created in Christ Jesus to do good works, which God prepared in advance for us to do.*"

–Ephesians 2:10

CHAPTER ONE

New York City, New York
April, 1968

"Hey, you're that girl ..." The woman's voice trailed off as she peered down her nose, squinting her eyes in scrutiny as she waved a bejeweled hand toward Elka. Her tone was more accusatory than friendly.

Elka ignored the statement, pretending she didn't hear. She forced a tight smile onto her face and picked up two menus. "Your table is ready, Mr. and Mrs. Smith. Jacob will be your waiter tonight." She motioned for them to follow her. "Right this way, please."

She led the couple through the oak-paneled dining room toward table nine. Thankfully, the Smiths were the last reservation of the night. After working in the Palm Court that afternoon, Elka had volunteered to cover a shift in the Biltmore's steak restaurant, the Guard Room. Due to illness, the regular host had bailed at the last minute. The extra money would be nice, but after ten hours on her feet, Elka was exhausted.

When they reached the table, she pulled out a red leather chair for the woman and waited for her to sit down. Mrs. Smith, who appeared to be around Elka's age—early-twenties—continued to stand. Smug satisfaction replaced her probing expression as she nudged her much-older husband with an elbow, then pointed. A similar scenario played out nearly every day. Elka knew what would come next.

"You're Elka Hansen. You were on the cover of Seventeen—several times." There was no point in denying it. Certainty beamed across the woman's face.

"Yes. That was a long time ago ..." An acknowledgment and a simple deflection toward another topic usually were enough to steer most people away from talking about Elka's past.

"And now you're working *here? As a hostess?*" The condescension dripped from Mrs. Smith's voice. Then the woman laughed dismissively before sitting down and picking up her menu, a smirk remaining on her face.

Elka, once again, ignored the woman, assuming her questions were rhetorical anyhow. It came with the territory. She tried to blend in, but people still recognized her.

After winning a modeling contest at fourteen, Elka had gained steady work as a catalog model. In 1963, at the age of sixteen, she began landing covers on teen magazines. That was when her father moved the whole family from Pennsylvania to New York so Elka would be closer to her work.

It had all been fun for a while, but Elka lost interest in modeling as she got older. Then the assignments tapered off and paid less. At eighteen, everything changed. She told her parents she wanted to quit modeling and go to college. They told her there was no money for school.

Elka had been financing her family's extravagant lifestyle the entire time they'd lived in New York. After that revelation, she'd remained close to her sister but not her parents. Her initial fury had subsided, but the hurt remained. Elka was on her own. Her parents had since moved to Connecticut, and she saw them only when necessary.

People seemed to expect a teenage "it" girl to lead a glamorous life, but Elka was no longer a teen, and the money she earned as a hostess at the Palm Court didn't seem to cover much beyond her rent at Morgan Hall, the Y.W.C.A. dormitory nearby. Her current lifestyle was a disappointment to some, and it was a source of pity or amusement to others. Elka did her best to brush it all away. It didn't matter what strangers thought.

Besides, she liked her job. Until she figured out exactly what it was she wanted to do with her life, Elka was happy enough, right where she was. She worked in a beautiful hotel, and though she'd started as a coat-check girl in the Palm Court, she'd recently received a promotion to hostess, breaking down a boundary at the Biltmore. Until then, the hotel had only hired men to work the dining rooms.

Mr. Smith, to his credit, seemed embarrassed by his wife's rude comments. He cleared his throat before giving Elka an apologetic smile. "Thank you, miss." He took his seat.

Elka gave a curt nod, handed over a menu, and quickly spun away on her heel, colliding into Jacob, who'd been standing behind her with a glass water pitcher. The waiter raised his arm gracefully, preventing any impact and further embarrassment from a spill. How much had he overheard?

"Pardon me." Elka avoided eye contact as her face heated. It was probably as red as the uniform jacket he wore. It was time to go home. As she walked away, Elka overheard Mrs. Smith's words.

"And to think, I once wanted to be like her. Oh, my, how the tables have turned!" A shriek soon followed those haughty words.

Erika spun around to see the cause of the commotion. Mrs. Smith's glass of water had somehow ended up soaking the front of her dress. Jacob jumped into action to help clean up the mess, but he threw Elka a glance, and a flash of mischief flickered across his handsome face.

The following morning a loud buzzing sound interrupted Elka's dream. Her hand reached out from the covers and slammed down on the snooze button without opening her eyes. Then she pulled the blanket back over her head. She had the next two days off and had slept late, but she needed to get up soon. Colleen would be waiting for her.

On Mondays, Elka took the subway from midtown to upper Manhattan to see her sister. They usually met for lunch at Finnigan's, a diner on 115th and Broadway. She was proud of her younger sister, a mathematics major on full scholarship at Barnard, and always looked forward to their time together.

This morning, Elka was having a hard time rousing herself. *I'll just throw my hair into a ponytail. That will give me a few more minutes of sleep.*

When the alarm buzzed again, she hit the clock radio for the final time and switched on the music. Joni Mitchell's "Both Sides Now" played. Elka loved the song and began humming along as she climbed out of bed. Moving aside the lace curtain hung above the desk, she opened her window and gazed down on the street below.

A warm breeze carried the aroma of fresh bagels from the deli across the street. The city was already awake—yellow cabs blasted their horns, and pedestrians moved about the crowded sidewalks like busy ants. Elka grabbed her pink chenille robe and pushed her feet into the matching slippers. Then she stepped out of her room and into the hallway, journeying toward the bathroom she shared with the other women on her floor. Most of them were already at work. At this hour, at least there wouldn't be a line to use the shower.

Forty-five minutes later, Elka rode the subway, absorbed in a story from the *New York Times*—another clash in Saigon—casualties on both sides. When the train stopped at the 116th Street station, she folded it up and stuffed it into her straw bag. Colleen was waiting for her when she walked up the stairs and onto the street.

"Hey—" Colleen's long dark hair bounced in loose waves around her shoulders as she hopped off the pony wall where she'd been sitting. She sported a black beret, identical to the one Elka wore. Thick, black-rimmed glasses rested low on the bridge of her nose, giving her the appearance of a child playing dress-up.

Colleen, who attended Barnard, was a young college student at eighteen, but her petite size and a smattering of freckles across her pert nose made her seem even younger. Elka was taller than her sister and didn't need glasses, but other than those minor differences, looking at Colleen was almost like staring into a mirror.

"Hey, Bugs! How's school?" Elka grinned and waved. The nickname came from her younger sister's love of cartoons—in particular, Bugs Bunny. As a girl, Elka had always enjoyed sleeping late when given a chance, but Colleen had rarely let that happen, insisting her older sister get up and watch early morning cartoons with her on Saturday mornings.

"School is going well. I have something to tell you, but let's wait 'till we get to Finnigan's." Colleen slung her book bag over her shoulder and began walking in the direction of the restaurant.

Fifteen minutes later, the sisters had already placed their lunch orders and were drinking coffee in their favorite booth by the window. Colleen reached into her bag, pulled out a flyer, and pushed it across the table toward Elka. The headline at the top of the paper read, "Stop Columbia's Gym Crow."

Elka read more, discovering the play on words referred to the new gym the university planned to build on land donated by the city. The property came from Morningside Park in Harlem. The nearby residents would lose much of their already limited green space, and the gym would be primarily restricted to Columbia students. A community group was petitioning against what they called a land grab. The flyer stated that the Sundial Rally would be held on Tuesday, April 23, at noon.

Elka could feel Colleen's eyes boring into her, waiting for her to finish reading. When Elka finally glanced up from the paper, her sister leaned across the table and took a deep breath.

"So, do you want to come back tomorrow and go to the rally with me?" Colleen asked, her tone sounding hopeful.

Elka admired her sister's activism and her passion for civil rights but the protests and rallies could also be dangerous. Elka didn't pray often, but when she did, requests were frequently related to her sister's safety. If she saw injustice, Colleen was more likely to run toward rather than away from the action. The city was still on edge from Martin Luther King Jr.'s assassination only three weeks ago. Who knew what could happen? Elka wanted to protect her sister.

"Okay, I'll come." The words escaped her lips before Elka even had a chance to think about them.

Elka moved over and made room on the seat for the old lady who'd boarded the subway on Seventy-Second Street. The woman, who smelled like peppermint, gave Elka a slight nod, then pulled a paperback novel out of a canvas tote and began reading. The lady didn't even look up when three men walked through their car, loudly singing, "Runaround Sue." They harmonized with impressive skill. When one of them held out his hat, Elka reached over and dropped a dime into it. That's when she spotted Jacob, the waiter from work.

He sat across the aisle and two seats in front of her. How had she not noticed Jacob there before? It was definitely him. There was no mistaking that strong jawline. Elka had never seen him wearing anything but his red waiter's uniform. Today he wore blue jeans and a black turtleneck sweater, and his dark hair was casually mussed instead of carefully styled with pomade, which was the way he wore it at work. A pretty blonde girl sat next to him. Probably his girlfriend.

Since they usually worked in different parts of the hotel, Elka didn't know much about Jacob. She'd only talked to him a couple of times, but over the past day or two, her mind kept wandering back to the incident with the spilled water. Did he do it on purpose? For her? She wondered where he lived and where he was going right now.

The pretty girl got off on 110th Street. So did the old lady. Jacob remained, but he still hadn't looked back or noticed her. When the train arrived at her stop, Jacob stood. Was he a student at Columbia? On the platform, they came face-to-face.

His smile, upon recognition of Elka, was friendly. "Hey, Elka! How are you? Finally got a day off, huh? What are you doing all the way out here?" His steps fell in line with Elka's, and he walked up the stairs with her.

"I'm meeting my sister. She's a student at Barnard. What about you?"

"Hmm, I'm at Columbia. Which way are you going?"

"The library. There's a rally today—"

"Well, that's where I'm going. Mind if I walk with you?"

Did she mind? Why did she feel like she had butterflies in her stomach? Elka felt an unfamiliar awkward feeling. Was it because Jacob was cute? She'd spent time with plenty of good-looking guys. What was wrong with her?

"Of course not. I'm glad we ran into each other." Elka smiled, doing her best to appear relaxed. When she saw Colleen walking toward them, Elka took a deep breath to center herself. Today wasn't going to be about flirting with cute guys. There was a deeper purpose to why she'd come—and she'd best remember that.

CHAPTER TWO

"Jacob ... good to see you!" Colleen said, just as Elka was about to introduce them.

How did Colleen know Jacob? Elka jerked her head back, and her sister laughed. "Wait, you two know each other?"

Jacob reached out his hand and gave Colleen a high five. "Elka and I both work at the Biltmore. And I take it you both know each other too." They were standing in the middle of a busy sidewalk, and pedestrians having to maneuver around them expressed irritation in various forms—grunts, glares, and bumps. "Okay, don't tell me ... you're sisters! Right? Hansen. Aha!" Jacob grinned. "I don't know why I didn't put that together sooner. You certainly look alike."

Elka could hear someone shouting over a bullhorn in the distance, though the words were hard to make out. She tucked a piece of hair behind her ear and smiled. "Hey, sis." Then she hugged Colleen to move her to the side of the sidewalk. "I think we're blocking traffic."

"Thanks for coming, Elka." Colleen made a motion for Elka to follow her, and they started walking toward the library. "I think we first met at an SDS meeting last winter. Is that right, Jacob?"

"Yes, I think that's right." Jacob fished out a pack of spearmint gum from his satchel and took a piece. Then he offered it to the girls. "Want some?"

Elka nodded and held out her hand. "Thank you. What's SDS?" As they got closer to the library, the crowd became denser. The air seemed to crackle with tension.

"Students for a Democratic Society. It's about anti-war stuff and civil rights issues, like this." Jacob waved an arm toward the sundial ahead.

A tall skinny guy wearing a Columbia Crew team sweatshirt walked over to their group. He seemed to know Colleen and Jacob. "The library is locked," he said. "The demonstration has moved to Morningside Park." The guy glanced at Elka and smiled. Then he held out his hand. "Hi, I'm Chase."

"Elka. Nice to meet you. We're going to the building site for the gym?" Elka asked. Chase nodded.

People in the area began shouting, "Gym Crow must go!" Counterdemonstrators were mixed in with the crowd too. Angry, intimidating young men hurled insults toward other students.

"Go home, pukes!" one burly man shouted.

"Ignore those jocks," Chase said. "They just want to stir up trouble."

Elka moved closer to her sister, who was now chanting with the group. The chanting wasn't Elka's thing, and she felt awkward. She looped her arm with Colleen's, feeling protective. They were now part of the crowd and moving in the direction of what, Elka assumed, was the building site. There must have been about five hundred students walking with them at this point.

By the time they reached the park, Elka and Colleen had lost track of Jacob and Chase. The excavation site was a massive and ugly scar that cut through the park. A chain-link barrier surrounded the dirt hole. A few students started to climb the fences, but four policemen stopped them. Elka couldn't see everything that was happening ahead, but she could hear people screaming, and she saw one kid being taken away in handcuffs. This wasn't what she'd expected at all.

The tension continued to mount until, finally, a voice over a bullhorn spoke out. The crowd quieted. "That's Mark Rudd," Colleen whispered. "He's the president of SDS here at Columbia."

Even though she tried hard to listen, Elka still couldn't make out what he was saying. She was getting hungry, so to keep her mind off her empty stomach, Elka occupied herself by observing the people around her. They didn't fit any single stereotype other than most appeared to be young students. Some of them held signs, while others like her, lent nothing more than their presence to the demonstration.

After some time, Rudd told the group of five hundred at the park to go back to the sundial to join up with more students. Elka searched the crowd to see if she could spot Jacob. She located him in the distance with Chase, but now they were moving again, and it was impossible to do anything except go with the flow.

Back at the sundial in front of Lowe Library, the crowd had grown. They'd gained the attention of the administration. Accompanied by police officers, several older people, who appeared to be faculty members, made their way toward Mark Rudd, the man with the megaphone. Minutes later, it appeared as if they were negotiating with him.

Elka had been on her feet for at least three hours now. She should have worn something other than sandals and a short dress. Why didn't her sister tell her what to wear? "Come on, let's find a place to sit," she said to her sister.

Colleen, who seemed more comfortable in blue jeans and sneakers, responded by plopping down right on the pavement in the middle of the walkway. The other activists who were around them did the same. Were they accomplishing anything with this demonstration? Elka wasn't sure, but she was glad she came. She believed in the cause, and wanted to support her sister. Until they found out what was happening next, there was nothing to do but wait.

"Hey, there's Jacob and Chase, over there." Colleen pointed toward the grass strip in front of the library. "The lawn will be more comfortable. Let's join them." She stood and began moving, making a path through the crowd. Elka followed.

Jacob waved when he saw Elka and Colleen coming toward him. He made room for the girls to sit. "So, I heard the plan now is that we're taking the demonstration inside, to Hamilton Hall."

The afternoon was getting away from her. Elka hadn't planned on spending the whole day at Columbia. She still needed to go to the laundromat if she wanted to have a clean uniform when she went to work in the morning. Maybe now would be a good time to bow out and go home. Colleen would be okay staying with Chase and Jacob. "Hey, Colleen, I think I might go now. Do you mind?"

"Of course not! Thanks for coming. I'll call you tomorrow and fill you in on whatever you missed." Colleen reached over and hugged Elka.

"Jacob, I'll see you around." Elka waved. "Chase, it was good to meet you."

"Don't be a stranger. Thanks for coming out and supporting our cause," Chase said.

Jacob stood. "I'll walk you back to the station."

Elka nodded, grateful for the offer. "Thank you." She tried to ignore the teasing wink her sister gave her and hoped Jacob didn't see. It wasn't like that. Jacob was a coworker, and that was all.

Elka paused in front of the revolving doors and looked up at the Biltmore stretching twenty-six stories into the sky, magnificent and stately. A breath caught in her chest for a moment. Beautiful buildings did that to her. She smiled and waved at Hank, one of the doormen on duty, and continued walking toward the service entrance farther down the block.

After five years of living in Manhattan, Elka finally considered herself a real New Yorker. The city was a part of her. She'd seen just about everything, and not much caused her to bat an eye anymore. Strolling or stopping in the middle of the sidewalk to gawk at the scenery was a tourist move, and Elka knew better, but sometimes, she couldn't help herself. It never got old. The pleasure of living and working amid such stunning beauty and art was a gift.

Once inside the building, Elka rushed to the employee elevator that led to the women's locker room on the top floor. Her shift at the Palm Court started at 11:00 a.m. sharp. It was already 10:50. Mr. Barrows, her boss, did not abide tardiness. The locker room was empty. Thank goodness, because there wasn't time for chitchat. After slipping out of her street clothes and into the mod black and white shift that was her uniform, Elka shoved her belongings into her locker. A glance in the mirror, a swipe of red lipstick, and she was ready to go downstairs.

The gold-figured clock in the lobby read 10:58.

"Good morning, Miss Hanson." Mr. Barrows eyed Elka sternly, then nodded toward the clock. "Cutting it a little close this morning?"

"Good morning, Mr. Barrows. I apologize—"

Her boss simply nodded and continued on his way toward the front desk. He could be gruff, but Elka liked the old gentleman. She knew his salty demeanor was merely a cover. Underneath that was a soft heart. He'd given her a chance by making her the first female hostess at the Biltmore, and for that, Elka was grateful. She'd moved up from checking the minks, chinchillas, Yorkies, and pugs of the *ladies who lunched* to taking their reservations and seating them. A few gentlemen dined in the Palm Court as well, but not many. Most of them went to the Men's Bar in the hotel.

Elka's new job came with a surprising amount of power—discretion and a thorough knowledge of New York society's hierarchy were absolute requirements. Though Mr. Barrows was the maitre'd in name, he delegated many of his responsibilities to Elka, and everyone knew it. It was a delicate tightrope to walk, knowing who to place at the most sought-after tables and which names took precedence with the hard-to-get reservations. The social climbers often tipped better than the queen bees, as they wanted to get into her good graces. Still, Elka had the restaurant's reputation to balance against her financial interests. If she let in too many *climbers*, the overall desirability of being seen at the Palm Court would diminish.

At her podium, Elka moved the phone and opened the black leather-bound book that held the reservations. Names like Onassis, Astor, Javitz, and Stein filled the pages. Who were the guests today? Which of the waitstaff was working? These questions were important.

The guests often requested specific waiters, particularly Jacques. He was undeniably handsome and charming, hence his popularity, but he couldn't take care of the whole room. And then, of course, the waiters all knew who the best tippers were, so naturally, they wanted Elka to place those guests at their tables. When she did, they often rewarded her with a share of their tips. Every little bit helped. Living in New York wasn't cheap. Being a person who guests and staff alike sought favors from made Elka's position both enjoyable and enviable. She had no complaints, except for the high heels she had to wear. Her shift had barely begun, yet even now, she could feel her feet protesting as the pointy toe box squeezed them tight.

Soon the phone would start ringing, and the first guests would begin arriving. But for now, the Palm Court remained quiet. Elka gazed around the grand room, seeking anything that might be out of place. Everything was perfect. The silver and the Baccarat stemware sparkled, artfully folded linen napkins awaited, and exquisite peony centerpieces added soft elegance to the tables. The star jewels of the room were the brass chandeliers hanging from the glass vaulted ceiling. The light, airy, feminine place of luxurious refinement felt a far cry from the dirty construction site at the park where Elka had spent the better part of yesterday. That thought led to more concerning the event.

How had the demonstration gone? Would she see Jacob again? She rarely saw him at work.

Elka pushed all thoughts of aching feet, demonstrations, and Jacob aside as the Palm Court came to life. The lunch crowd was arriving now, fresh from the beauty salon. It was like a fashion show—Dior, Chanel, Oscar de la Renta, Saint Laurent. These ladies were always prepared for the swarm of photographers waiting outside the Biltmore's doors.

For the next few hours, Elka was wholly absorbed in meeting her customers' needs. High maintenance was the name of the game with these people, and Lady Westingford was today's prime example. The woman was a former actress, not an aristocrat. Nevertheless, she insisted on using the title. She came in around noon with a couple of friends and proceeded to send her soup back three times, claiming it wasn't hot enough. She also complained that her ice water wasn't cold enough. Marco, her waiter, was exceedingly patient and accommodated all her demands. Yet when Lady Westingford left, instead of a tip, she left behind her autograph. After that, Elka had to sweet-talk poor Marco into staying. He was so angry he'd threatened to walk out in the middle of his shift.

By four o'clock, with the last of the tables cleared out, Elka was ready for her break. She decided to use one of the pay phones in the lobby to call her sister. Colleen was usually in her room at this time. Not today. Nothing but ringing. A smidge of worry clawed at the back of Elka's mind. *Maybe the newspaper will have something to say about the demonstration at Columbia.* There were always papers laying around upstairs in the employee lounge.

After she stepped out of the elevator, Elka took off her heels and carried them as she made her way to the break room. That felt good. The top two floors of the hotel were for employees only. Some of them lived here. The demand for these rooms was high, which was why Elka was still on the waiting list.

She took a shortcut through the pool area, not seeing the puddle of water on the floor until it was too late, and she slipped. As Elka lunged forward and tried to catch herself, she put her foot down and felt a sickening snap around her ankle.

Ouch! Why am I so clumsy? The lounge was just down the hallway. *I'll put some ice on it, and it will be fine.* But when she tried to put weight on her right foot, a sharp pain shot through her entire body.

CHAPTER THREE

Jacob Lewis hoped the employee lounge would be empty. He needed some uninterrupted study time before his shift started. There wasn't any need to be downstairs for another forty-five minutes, and his books were here, ready to crack open. Whenever he could—on the subway or during breaks at work—Jacob took advantage of nearly every opportunity he had to fit in schoolwork. It was his last term before law school. If he got into law school. He was still waiting to find out. If he didn't get in, well, Jacob didn't want to even think about that. He'd probably need to go to Viet Nam. Staying in school was a way to avoid the draft, but graduation was in just a few weeks.

Last night, Jacob would ordinarily have been in his dorm room, studying, but instead, he'd been at Hamilton Hall. The previous day's demonstration at his school had turned into a sit-in, and then, an occupation. He'd stuck around until close to five-thirty in the morning, which was when the group had splintered. There had been some tension over the students' different purposes for being there.

The Student Afro-American Society (SAS) wanted to stay focused on their original goal—protesting the new gym. They asked everyone else, many of whom were there to protest the war, and Columbia's involvement, to leave Hamilton Hall. Jacob knew some of the newly evicted students were planning to occupy some of the other buildings at Columbia and continue protesting, but he couldn't afford to miss class or work.

The split had been his cue to leave. Now, after thirty-plus hours of being awake, Jacob was dog-tired. Only multiple cups of strong coffee, and some equally strong determination, were keeping him on his feet. He just hoped he'd be able to remember his customers' dinner orders tonight.

Only one person occupied the lounge when Jacob entered. She was standing on one foot, getting ice cubes out of the freezer. When Elka turned toward him, Jacob decided he could put off studying a bit longer.

She gave him a weak smile. "Oh, hey, Jacob ..." Elka seemed to grimace with pain as she put the ice into a bag, then she limped over to the couch.

"What happened? Are you hurt?" Dumb question. She couldn't even walk.

"I'll be okay. I was clumsy, and I slipped on a step. After I ice my ankle, I should be fine." Elka winced as she put the bag of ice on her right ankle that was already taking on a purplish hue.

"Is there anything I can do for you? Maybe you should go to the hospital and have that checked out—"

"No, no—" Elka looked at the clock on the wall, then frowned. Then she tried to put her shoe on. Her foot was too swollen. It wasn't going to happen. There was no way it was going to fit. She sighed, then finally conceded. "I don't think I'm going to be able to finish my shift tonight."

"No, I don't think so either." Jacob wanted to help, but he wasn't sure how. There was something about Elka that brought out the protective, older-brother side of him. Or was it more than that? She was a sweet girl and undeniably gorgeous, with deep-chocolate-brown eyes that seemed to hold a hint of sadness. He'd heard the rumors about her having been some kind of famous model, but her friendly, easy-going personality made her approachable. And based on her presence at yesterday's protest, Jacob surmised that she was more than just a pretty face. She cared about social justice for one thing.

"I guess I should call Mr. Barrows and let him know what happened." Elka got off the couch and hopped on one foot toward the phone on the wall. Jacob nodded, then fished around in his book bag for Tylenol. When he found the bottle, he put it on the coffee table and moved toward the sink to get her some water. How was she going to get home if she couldn't walk?

After Elka finished her phone call, she hopped back toward the couch. She smiled when she saw the Tylenol. "Thank you."

Jacob handed Elka a glass of water. "No problem. Do you have a way to get home—other than hopping?"

"I live close. I'll be fine. Between the Tylenol and the ice, I'm sure I can make it after a few minutes of resting. I have a different pair of shoes in my locker." Elka glared at the high heels on the floor with an air of distaste.

"Let me help you. At least let me call a cab." Jacob checked the clock. He still had a few minutes to spare.

"That's kind of you, but I promise I'll be okay." Elka reached for the newspaper laying on the coffee table. "So, what happened yesterday at Columbia after I left?"

Jacob told Elka about his sleepless night and the sit-in at Hamilton Hall. He explained how some students had trapped Dean Coleman inside his office for a time and said the group separated in the morning, only to go on to occupy even more buildings. He finished by explaining how he wished he could have stayed. "I think they're in for the long haul. If this is what it takes to get their attention ..."

Elka's face turned white. "Do you know if my sister stayed? I tried calling her, and she didn't answer."

"She might have been with the group that went to Low Library. Do you want me to check on her?"

"Yes, please. I'd appreciate it. I'm all for the cause, but I worry about Colleen."

"I get it. I have two younger sisters myself. They're both in Seattle."

"Is that where you're from, Seattle?" Elka asked.

Jacob nodded. "Born and raised there. How about you? Where are you from?"

"Pittsburgh. I moved here when I was sixteen." Elka took the ice bag off her ankle and inspected her foot. "I'm going to go change out of my work clothes and make my way home. It was nice chatting with you. I'm sure this ankle will feel better in the morning. I plan on being at work tomorrow. If you get word of my sister, would you mind stopping by the Palm Court and letting me know?" She moved to get off the couch, but when she tried to put weight on her right foot, she gasped in pain.

Jacob jumped up and offered Elka his arm. "Here, lean on me. I'll go downstairs with you and help you get a cab." This time, she didn't argue.

The view from Jacob's second-floor single at Livingston Hall overlooked the Van Am Quadrangle. It was a beautiful spring day, and though it was still early, the campus was already beginning to awaken. Students walked on the paths below. From here, it seemed like a regular Thursday, but Jacob knew it wasn't. Would there be classes today? He still had an hour before he needed to be at Philosophy Hall.

After returning from work last night, three gruff law officers had blocked the pathway onto campus, asking for his identification. Jacob first had to prove he had a right to be there before being allowed back to his dorm. This kind of thing had never happened before, and it left him feeling unsettled. According to Michael, his buddy across the hall, not only were students still occupying Low and Hamilton, but more of them had moved into Avery Hall as well.

He'd promised Elka to check on her sister, Colleen, so he'd walk over to the library and see what he could find out. Thinking about Elka made him smile. His job at the Biltmore was more fun now. He relished the possibility of running into the new hostess from the Palm Court. Hopefully, her recent injury wouldn't keep her away for too long.

Before exiting his building, he stopped by the post office boxes to see if he had any mail. The sight of one white envelope, with a return address that included Columbia Law, made Jacob's heart race. His hand was shaky as he hurriedly tore into the paper, ripping the letter out as fast as he could.

Dear Mr. Lewis:
We regret to inform you ...

Jacob crumpled the letter in frustration, his good mood vanished. He hadn't yet received replies from Seattle University, NYU, or Gonzaga—the other three law schools he'd applied to—but this first rejection stung, and his confidence had taken a hit. Would his school be on the east or the west coast? Jacob wanted to stay in New York, but any option sounded better than Nam.

"Hey, Jacob, did you get breakfast yet? I was just on my way to the dining hall—" Michael, standing nearby, interrupted his thoughts.

Jacob shoved the letter into his satchel. Usually, he skipped breakfast in favor of a few extra minutes of sleep, but the idea occurred to him that one way to support the cause of his friends who were protesting would be to take them some food. They must be hungry, and delivering food would provide an excellent excuse to check on Colleen. Jacob looked at Michael, who was still waiting for an answer. Maybe he'd be willing to help. "No, I haven't. I'll come with you."

Michael, who was wearing a mysterious green armband, led the way. As they walked toward the dining hall, Jacob noticed several other students wearing armbands—some red, some blue, others green like Michael's.

"What's that about?" Jacob pointed toward his friend's arm.

"Oh, the armband?" Michael grinned. "Man, you missed out on a lot while you were at work yesterday. Green means I want amnesty for the protestors."

Jacob nodded. "And what do the other colors mean?"

"Red is what the protestors are wearing. Blue means you're against the protestors. Some of the faculty are wearing white armbands. They want a peaceful resolution. And black? I'm not sure what that color means."

"Ah, ha." They were outside the dining hall now. The smell of burnt coffee wafting from the building assaulted Jacob's nostrils. If he wanted good coffee, he'd need to go elsewhere. But maybe he could talk Ida, the cashier, into sending a few extra pieces of fruit and some donuts with him. Through the window, Jacob could see the older woman at her usual station.

"Let me see what I can do, honey." Ida smiled and gave Jacob's hand a maternal pat after listening to his request. "Go on, eat your breakfast, but come back and see me again before you leave."

A few minutes later, when he returned, Ida had packed two brown paper bags with food for him to take. "Take it all. It's on the house," she said, smiling. "Just some old leftovers ..."

"This is very generous. Thank you." Jacob smiled back. Ida's kindness was like an injection of hope.

Michael had to get to his first class of the day, so Jacob schlepped the groceries to Low Library by himself. He wasn't sure if Colleen would be there or how he would get the food to the protestors inside. Would they just let him walk inside like a delivery boy? How did this kind of thing work?

A police cordon surrounded the front of Low Library. Jacob felt momentarily defeated, but then he decided to walk around to the side of the building. It was clear.

"Jacob!" a voice called to him. It was Chase, leaning out the window from the second story.

"You hungry? I brought food." Jacob got straight to the point. He was going to be late for his first class if he didn't hurry. "How can I get these bags to you?"

A voice spoke from behind. "Here, I'll take them inside. Thanks, man!"

Jacob turned to see a skinny kid with a mop of red hair standing near him. He looked up toward Chase, who nodded with approval. Jacob handed over the bags and watched as the kid proceeded to climb through an open window on the first floor, just as naturally as if he'd been using the front door.

"Hey, Chase, is Colleen Hansen in there?" Jacob asked his friend.

"Yeah, she's right here."

Just then, Colleen appeared at the window and waved to Jacob. She gave him a thumbs up.

He returned the gesture. Good. She was okay—for now. But what was the plan in all this? How would it end?

Elka tried to call her sister again on Thursday morning. Still no answer. Hanging up the phone, she let out a deep sigh. Colleen was always in her room at this early hour, usually still asleep. If she wasn't there now, then it was logical to assume she hadn't slept there last night. And if that was the case, Elka was sure that Colleen was with the protesters occupying several Columbia buildings.

Admiration, combined with fear over her sister's current situation, made Elka shiver— or maybe it was the breeze coming from the open window at the end of the hallway. She limped over and closed it. Colleen had strong ideals and was selfless, continually doing good things for other people with little regard for the consequences. Elka wished she could be more carefree and idealistic like that.

Instead, her personality was practical, and she worried about boring things, like paying the rent and keeping her sister out of trouble. Elka felt aimless. What *did* she want to do with her life? She loved her sister too much to be jealous, but it would be nice to have a stronger sense of purpose like Colleen seemed to have.

Colleen was probably okay right now. Maybe her sister didn't need her "help." Their parents didn't seem to be concerned with how either of them was faring. They'd become hands-off parents as soon as any financial or social benefits that came from being involved in their daughters' lives had ceased. Elka's feelings toward them vacillated between hurt and anger, but she did her best to push those feelings away, as she did now. There were other matters to ponder.

Her sore ankle had made the short walk from her room to use the phone challenging. It couldn't be broken—probably just swollen. When she'd gone to sleep last night, Elka had hoped her injury would be better in the morning. She couldn't miss work. More accurately, she couldn't miss the paycheck that came from working. Maybe Mr. Barrows would be able to move her to another job in the hotel that didn't require so much walking? She hoped so. Hurrying back to her room, Elka decided to go to work early and talk with her boss. She was at the mercy of Mr. Barrows, and she'd need his favor to keep her job.

Elka finished getting ready. As she brushed her hair, she thought about Jacob's kindness, helping her downstairs and into a cab last night. He was charming, a real gentleman. They were coworkers, but they'd never even had a conversation until last week, but somehow, over these past few days, he'd come to her rescue several times. Though she'd been in pain and embarrassed at her clumsiness, Jacob's attention toward her had been a bright spot in what would have, otherwise, been a terrible evening.

Elka left through the front doors of Morgan Hall ten minutes later and hailed a cab. It was a splurge with her tight budget, but what else could she do? It wasn't far to the Biltmore, and there was no point in being a martyr, at least not yet. *New York is a walking city. I cannot afford to be hobbling around for long. Oh, what am I going to do?*

Mr. Barrows was in his office when Elka arrived. The door was ajar, and she could see that he was reading a newspaper at his desk. She gave a little knock. "Mr. Barrows? May I speak with you?"

He put the paper down and waved her in. The room was fastidiously tidy, much like its primary occupant, and furnished with a few well-chosen antiques—a mahogany desk, a matching bookshelf, and two dark green leather swivel chairs. A large window behind her boss's desk framed a view of Grand Central Terminal across the street.

"Miss Hansen, come in, have a seat. How's the ankle?" Mr. Barrows frowned as he watched Elka limp into his office. "Should you be walking on that? Have you seen a doctor?"

"I think it will be fine in a few days, but I'm not sure I'll be able to work my shift in the Palm Court ..." Elka didn't want to admit that she had no way to pay for a doctor's visit.

"No, I think not. Don't worry about that. I'll find someone to cover you." Mr. Barrows opened a drawer in his desk and shuffled some items around until he found what he was searching for —a business card. He handed it to Elka. "Dr. Peterson has an office just around the corner. Tell him I sent you. The hotel will cover any expenses since you were hurt here at work."

Technically, she'd been on a break, but why argue? "Thank you." Elka tucked the card into the purse on her lap. She hesitated and cleared her throat. "Mr. Barrows ... is there anywhere else in the hotel I could work ... in the meantime ... while my ankle is healing, a place where I wouldn't need to be on my feet so much?"

"I'll look into it. Maybe Ms. Anton could use your help at the front desk. Go, get that ankle checked out, see what the doctor says, and come back here when you're done. We'll take it from there."

Elka smiled with gratitude and stood to leave. "You're very kind." She couldn't imagine any former employers from her modeling days being so accommodating.

"You're a Biltmore Girl, and here, we take care of our own."

Getting an X-ray and then a cast on her foot had taken much longer than Elka had anticipated. *Broken ... six weeks* were not the words she'd wanted to hear from Dr. Peterson. It was nearly two in the afternoon, and hunger pains gnawed at her. She'd already skipped breakfast. These crutches were going to take some getting used to. How was she going to carry her tray at the automat? There was only one way to find out.

Elka walked into Horn and Hardart and surveyed the wall of vending machines. Baked goods, pies, sandwiches, each section was marked with a sign overhead. Elka leaned her crutches against the wall, out of the way, then hobbled over to an area where thick pieces of dark chocolate cake beckoned from behind the individual glass doors. She stood awkwardly on one leg as she reached for her purse, searched for a nickel, put it in a slot, and got her treat. A sandwich would have been sensible, but a piece of chocolate cake was sometimes necessary to turn a bad day around.

"Please, let me help you, miss," An older man with a gentle smile and eyes that twinkled stood next to her. "Where's your table? I'll carry that for you."

Accepting help from strangers was another thing she was going to have to get used to. "Thank you. I was just going to sit over there." Elka pointed to a table nearby with two empty chairs. She handed him her plate, and he set it on his tray next to his pie. He seemed to be alone. "You're welcome to join me if you like."

"Don't mind if I do, thank you. I was going to get some coffee to go with my pie. May I get some for you too?" He was a sweet man.

Twenty pleasant minutes passed too quickly as Elka and Mr. Sawyer sat together in the automat, chatting about everything and nothing in particular. Elka learned that he was a retired police officer and a recent widower. It was with genuine regret when she glanced at the clock on the wall and realized it was time to get back to the Biltmore. "I hope I'll see you around again sometime soon." She smiled at the gentleman.

"It was a pleasure to meet you, Elka. Hold on. I'll get your crutches for you."

Bolstered by a little kindness, sugar, and caffeine, Elka made her way back outside to Forty-Second Avenue.

Elka was grateful when she entered the Biltmore's lobby and spotted Mr. Barrows near the concierge desk. She wouldn't have to search for him. The lunch crowd was probably tapering off at this hour in the Palm Court. She wondered who was covering her shift.

Mr. Barrows glanced her way, taking in the cast and crutches. "Ah, Miss Hansen, there you are. Broken?" She nodded. He frowned in commiseration. "Well, Ms. Anton can use your help at the front desk. You'll be able to stay in one place, at least. Though, I'll miss having you in the Palm Court." He straightened his tie. "Talk to her. She'll get you started."

Elka approached the front desk. Ms. Anton, her new boss, was helping a customer, so Elka chose a silk settee to rest on while she waited.

Jacob spotted her and sauntered over. "Elka, how are you? I was looking for you in the Palm Court."

"Oh, well, here I am. I'll be working at the front desk for the next few weeks while this heals." She pointed to her cast.

"You're a tough one ... walking on that injury. Broken?"

"Yes, unfortunately. It's an inconvenient time." Elka brushed her hand through the air as if attempting to sweep away the problem itself. "Did you find out any news about my sister?"

Jacob nodded and sat next to Elka. "I saw her this morning. She's with the group at Low Library." He gave her a reassuring smile and touched her hand. "Hey, she seemed happy to be there. She was with friends. She's okay—don't worry."

"Aha, well ... thank you." This wasn't the right place to be having this particular conversation, and Ms. Anton was ready to see her now. Elka moved her crutches in preparation to get up.

"Here, let me help you." Jacob stood, then offered his hand to assist her in standing. They were close only for a brief moment, but as she took his hand, Elka noticed a subtly woodsy scent to his cologne. It was nice. "I'd like to talk some more. I'll find you at a better time."

Elka nodded. She wanted to know more about what was going on at Columbia. "That'd be good. I'd like that. I'll see you around." She smiled.

Jacob waved goodbye and walked over to the bank of elevators. Elka made her way over to the other side of the room to speak with her new boss. Ms. Anton, the front desk manager, wore her gray hair in a severe bun. A pair of wire-rimmed glasses with a chain attached to them and a black blazer added to an overall appearance that said *librarian*. A ready smile and a pink rose pinned on her lapel softened the look and made her more approachable.

"Ah, Miss Hansen. I hear you're joining my team for the time being. Welcome!" Ms. Anton said. Over the next few minutes, the woman gave Elka a quick overview of her new job, and she learned that she could start the next day at 7:00 a.m. Relief came over Elka, as one part of the burden she'd been carrying today had been lifted.

After Elka said goodbye to Ms. Anton, she glanced at the big clock in the lobby, trying to decide whether to take the elevator up to the employee lounge or go straight home. She wanted to find Jacob and ask about her sister, but she was also tired.

While she was standing there, contemplating what to do next, her mother walked through the front door and spotted her immediately. Elka felt a headache coming on.

As her mother marched nearer, her over-plucked eyebrows shot up. She pointed toward the clunky cast and Elka's foot.

"What happened to you?"

CHAPTER FIVE

The Guard Room wouldn't be welcoming its first diners for more than an hour. Jacob checked his watch. He had time to go to the loading dock and shoot the breeze with Terry and Carlos. The two cooks were usually out there at this time of day, smoking, gossiping, and joking around.

Jacob found both men right where he expected, but it was evident right away that something was wrong. Terry gave a half-hearted wave with one hand and rubbed out his cigarette with the other. "Hey, man. How's it going?" Terry sounded sad.

"Terry. Carlos. What's up?" Jacob sat on an overturned crate.

Carlos pried the cap off a bottle of Coke and took a long gulp. "We're going out for drinks after work if you want to come. It's Terry's last night."

Jacob was surprised. Terry had always seemed like someone who enjoyed his job. "Your last night? Oh, man. Why's that?"

"Nam. I signed up. I figured it was better to enlist than wait to be drafted." Terry shrugged.

"I'm going to Fort Dix on Monday—eight weeks."

Jacob frowned. "I'll miss seeing you around." Then, trying to lighten the mood, he said, "If they're smart, they'll take you on as a cook. You're one of the best!"

"Yeah, man ... I don't think the menu over there will include too much steak." Terry smiled.

The gray sky was starting to deliver on its promise. Cold, biting drops of rain began to fall. Why did Terry have to go? His friend was a gentle soul, happiest in the kitchen. He wanted to own a restaurant someday. He wasn't a fighter. So many good guys—heck, it seemed like half his graduating class was in Nam, fighting a war that none of them really understood. Was it the right thing to do, staying in college, to avoid a draft? He didn't know. It didn't seem fair that guys like Terry didn't seem to have much choice.

"I'm telling you, it's better to enlist. Don't wait to be drafted," Terry said. "At least, then, you might have more choice in where you end up." It wasn't the first time Jacob had heard such sentiments. With graduation so close and no concrete plans for what he was doing next, was he being foolish with his *wait and see* approach?

A produce truck pulled up to the dock. Carlos and Terry moved to assist the driver with unloading the freight. Jacob walked back toward the kitchen door to go inside. "Count me in for drinks later. Where are we going?"

"O'Malley's," Carlos answered. "See you later!"

Once inside, Jacob got to work. He checked the board to see what the specials were on his way through the kitchen. Then he wandered over to the front podium, where Antoine, one of the hosts, was scribbling something on a notepad. Jacob wanted to see if any of his favorite customers had reservations that night.

Every line on the page was full. It was going to be a busy evening, and that was more than okay with Jacob. He didn't want to dwell on things like war, getting into law school, or what would happen to his friends who were protesting at Columbia right now. All he wanted to think about was keeping up with his customers' dinner orders for the next few hours and bringing home a pocket full of tips.

Jacob was deep in thought as the subway brought him closer to midtown on Saturday morning. The expression on Elka's face when

Jacob informed her that Colleen was one of the protestors occupying Low Library had been one of horror. He'd been with her, only moments after she'd broken her ankle, but her reaction to that incident had paled in comparison to her response to the news he'd given her in the lobby regarding her sister. Her reaction was something he could respect and relate to. Jacob's own sisters evoked the same fierce protectiveness in him. Elka was a tough girl when it came to her own problems, but she obviously had a soft heart when it came to her sister.

Jacob was surprised to learn that Elka didn't have a personal phone—or maybe she'd only told him that because she wasn't interested in talking to him outside of work. He wasn't sure, though he hoped this wasn't the case. There was something compelling about this girl, and he wanted to get to know her better.

On Friday, Jacob stopped by the front desk to see if Elka was around. She was already gone, so he left a note, asking if she'd like to get lunch with him at The Oyster Bar on Saturday. As an afterthought, he'd added a postscript, letting her know how Colleen was doing and jotted down his phone number.

Elka returned Jacob's call early Saturday morning. It had been a rushed call. She needed to leave for work soon, but she said she had an hour for lunch at one o'clock.

Now, as the train hurtled through the dark tunnels, getting closer to his stop, Jacob realized he'd used the situation with Elka's sister as an excuse to score a date with her. Or was it a date? And if it was, should he feel guilty about that? He'd gone by Low Library this morning to check on his friends, Colleen included, and he'd delivered another bag of food to them. The protestors were still holding out, but the stand-off was tense, and nobody was sure how it would all end.

Getting off at the stop nearest the Biltmore, Jacob looked at his watch as he ascended the steps to the street. Twelve-fifty—right on time. When he entered the Biltmore lobby, Elka made eye contact with him and gave a slight nod from across the room. She was with a customer, so he decided he'd wait by the clock.

The Oyster Bar was across the street, inside Grand Central Terminal on the lower level. Jacob had tried to pick someplace close since Elka was on crutches, and he'd asked around to make sure they'd quickly find an elevator. He hoped she'd like his choice.

Elka soon joined Jacob under the clock. Unlike two days ago, now she seemed to move with ease on her crutches. The black blazer worn as a uniform by all the desk clerks had been replaced with a blue cardigan. To alleviate difficulty, she wore a long-handled crochet bag across her body instead of a normal handbag.

"Are you ready?" Elka poked him in the leg with the tip of her crutch and grinned. "I've been thinking about The Oyster Bar all morning. I love that place. Let's go."

Jacob smiled back. "Yeah, I'm ready."

The restaurant's tables, with their signature red-checkered tablecloths, were all occupied when they arrived. When offered a seat at the bar instead of a table, Elka didn't seem the least perturbed. She was a good sport. He liked that about her. After getting a Coke and an iced tea, they ordered two bowls of New England clam chowder.

Munching on oyster crackers while waiting, Elka got straight to the point. "My sister called me yesterday. It was good to hear from her, but she said she was going back to the library. To some extent, it seems she comes and goes as she pleases, using a window instead of the front door to exit the building." Elka scrunched up her nose. "Then she told me she even went to one of her classes." She sighed. "I admire her resolve, but what do you think is going to happen? Are those students in danger?"

"There are cops all over the campus right now. I've heard the administration is divided on what to do to bring an end to this. I really don't know ..." Jacob buttered a piece of bread while talking. He was concerned, but he didn't want to show it.

"I'm glad Colleen is still going to her classes. She's on a full-ride scholarship. Did she tell you that?" The pride in Elka's voice was unmistakable. She laughed. "I probably sound more like her mom than her sister." Elka rolled her eyes.

Jacob thought it was sweet. "I didn't know that, but I'm not surprised. She's smart."

Elka took a sip of her iced tea. "My mother came by the Biltmore the other day. She told me she was in the city—just stopping by to say hello—which she never does. Then she wanted to know why she couldn't get in touch with Colleen. I didn't know what to tell her."

She added a packet of sugar to the tea and stirred it. "I'm sure she read about the protests in the papers. I think she knows Colleen is involved." Elka shook her head and scrunched up her nose. "But I'm talking too much. What's new with you?"

A waiter brought their chowder. Hot steam wafted from the bowls, and it smelled delicious. "Well, I'm graduating in a month, and I'm not sure what comes after that. I've applied to a few law schools ..."

"Oh, yeah? What school is top of your list?"

"Columbia was, but I didn't get in." Jacob couldn't believe he'd just blurted that out. What if she thought he was a loser? He watched her face closely for her reaction. A gentle nod. Acceptance, not pity. He liked her even more.

"Ah, well. There are other good law schools. Are you staying in the city this summer?"

"I'd like to. I'm on the waiting list for employee housing at the Biltmore. I'm hoping something opens up there soon. Otherwise, I'll go back to Seattle."

Elka took another bite of her chowder then put her spoon down. "I hope that too—for you." She relaxed into the back of her chair.

Until a few days ago, Jacob would have been happy, one way or the other, but now staying in the city over the summer—or longer—was starting to take on greater importance. Elka Hansen intrigued him, and he wanted the opportunity to get to know her better. That would never happen if he went back to Seattle.

After his lunch with Elka, Jacob had a couple of hours to kill until he needed to start his shift. He was feeling more upbeat after spending time with her than he'd felt in a long while. Jacob was already thinking about when he might see her again. It was unfortunate that his shift always started just as Elka's ended. Their opposing schedules were a bummer. He'd use his free time now to stop by the human resources office and check on the housing list. It was posted on a bulletin board and updated once a week.

Jacob scanned the names and found his own. It didn't seem promising with five names ahead of his. If he wanted to stay in New York that summer—if he wanted to see Elka—he would have to come up with a different plan.

CHAPTER SIX

Elka owed her mother a call. The least she could do was let her know that Colleen was okay. She'd been vague when her mother had shown up without warning at the Biltmore. Elka had only relayed that she'd spoken to her sister on Tuesday, and her mother shouldn't worry because Colleen was just really busy right now with school. At the time, it was at least partly true. But now, she'd heard from Colleen once more.

It was as good a time as ever to make that call. Elka read the phone message, scribbled on a piece of paper, and slipped under her door by Sarah, the girl across the hall. Since all the women on this floor shared the one phone in the hallway, they often took messages for each other. This one was from Colleen.

Sorry I can't make it to lunch tomorrow.
I'll miss our time together.
All is well. See you next week.

Elka would miss their weekly lunch date, but at least she wouldn't have to try to navigate the subway with crutches. Now that she thought about it, Elka realized that her sister didn't even know she'd broken her ankle. During their brief conversation, she'd never told Colleen.

It didn't ease her anxiety much, but at least she knew Colleen was okay. And though the note didn't say so, Elka suspected the reason her sister couldn't make it was because she was still at Low library. The protest had been going on for almost a week. The longer it went on, the greater Elka's concern grew.

Colleen had not been in touch with their mother, and Elka understood that their mother really did care in her own strange way—or at least she hoped that was true. Picking up the receiver, Elka took a deep breath and dialed the number. A part of her wished it would just ring, and she could ease her guilt, knowing she'd tried, without actually needing to speak with her mother. And she *really* hoped her father wouldn't pick up.

"Doug Hansen speaking." No such luck.

"Hello, Father. How are you?" She forced herself to be cordial, even though the sound of his voice brought back all the betrayal and hurt. She felt her heart begin to pound a little faster.

"Hello, just fine. I'll put your mother on the phone." And with that, she heard him set down the phone.

Relief washed over her as she waited a few more moments, listening to the sounds of her father calling out to her mother, as desperate to avoid a conversation with his oldest daughter as she was with him.

"Elka. Hello." Mother's voice had that high pitch Elka recognized, the one she used when she was trying to pretend everything was fine. "What's going on? Have you talked to Colleen lately?"

"Yes, I talked to her a couple of days ago. She's fine." Elka twisted the phone cord into a tight coil.

"She's involved with those dirty hippies, isn't she? The ones trying to take over the campus."

"She's with good people, Mother. I've met her friends. There's nothing to worry about." Of course, Elka was concerned, but it didn't seem necessary to admit it.

Cisco, the resident orange tabby—who belonged to everyone and to no one—wandered over. He hopped onto Elka's lap. The cat always seemed to know when he was needed. Elka rested her hand on his soft, warm body and relaxed at the sound of his purring.

"Well, your father and I are leaving for Florida in the morning. We'll be gone for a few weeks. Please keep an eye on your sister."

"Of course. Have a good time." After a couple more minutes of stilted conversation, her mother said goodbye. Elka hung up the phone, and then it occurred to her that neither of her parents had bothered to ask about her life.

Elka had the rest of the day to herself, and it was only nine o'clock. The problem was how to get around the city on a broken ankle? Just making it up and down the stairs in her building felt challenging enough. She needed something close by that she could do.

She peered out her window and down onto the street below. Across from Morgan Hall was the Children's Aid Society. Elka enjoyed watching the children and their mothers coming and going from the building. Sarah, the girl across the hall, worked as a teacher there in the Head Start preschool. Maybe they could use some help. It wouldn't hurt to ask. She could go there today.

An hour later, Elka found herself sitting in a busy office, filling out paperwork in the old brick building that had served thousands of children since the middle of the nineteenth century.

"What hours are you available to volunteer?" Mrs. Nadington, the director, was sitting on the other side of her big oak desk, looking over the form Elka had just given her.

"I work at the Biltmore until three every day but Mondays and Tuesdays. Anytime outside of that, I'm free."

Behind Mrs. Nadington, a window gave view to the children playing outside in the courtyard. "We have an after-school program here, where children come in to get help with their homework. Is that something you would be interested in?" Mrs. Nadington pursed her lips.

Elka hadn't been the best student—not like her sister. She'd tried, but she'd missed a lot of school when she was modeling. Was she even qualified for this job? "Yes, I would like that very much."

"All right then. Can you come in at three today?" The director raised her eyebrows.

"Yes, I can."

Elka blew out a long breath and smiled when she left. *Hopefully, I'll have something to offer these kids.* She'd sensed some skepticism from Mrs. Nadington, so Elka set a resolution. *I'm not going to mess this up. I'll show her.*

"Elka!" a familiar voice called out from behind her. "Elka!"

"Hey, Jacob. Do you have the day off too?" Elka, who'd been on her way back to Morgan Hall, smiled at her friend and moved closer to the building so she could stop and talk.

"Yeah, I do. I was just viewing an apartment for rent across the street. Do you live around here?"

"Right here." Elka pointed toward the doorway they were standing near. "I take it you're staying in the city for the summer then?"

"If all goes well, maybe. I left an application." Jacob paused. "Hey, what are you doing right now? Do you have time to get lunch?"

Twice, in one week? Or maybe he's just hungry and wants some company.

Elka peeked at her watch. Noon. She still had three hours until she needed to be back at the Children's Aid Society. She smiled, shrugged, and looked down at her crutches. "As long as it's somewhere close. What did you have in mind?"

A green sightseeing bus parked across the street seemed to catch his attention. A crowd of people milled about, waiting to get on. He grinned and pointed at the vehicle. "How about we pretend we're tourists and go for a ride first? Then I'll buy you a hotdog in the park."

That did sound like a lot of fun. *Why not?* "Okay. I'm in!"

Elka enjoyed spending time with Jacob, and she had never been on a bus tour in all the time she'd lived here. The bus doors opened, and Elka contemplated how she would maneuver the three steps to get on.

"Here, hop on my back, and I'll carry those crutches for you," Jacob said.

She felt a little self-conscious, but what else was she going to do? Elka laughed and accepted the piggyback ride, feeling her cheeks grow warm. But she didn't mind being so close to him, for that brief moment. It was nice. Once on-board, Jacob insisted on paying for her ticket. Was this a date?

They were invited to sit at the bus's front because of Elka's cast. The driver took them through Manhattan as the tour guide pointed out familiar places—New York Public Library, Bryant Park, St. Patrick's Cathedral, and the Empire State Building. Elka was learning all sorts of fun things about her city, the kind of trivial facts that she enjoyed, such as the term, "Big Apple" came from the name of a local newspaper's horse racing column in the 1920s. "Big Apple" described big prize money. Their guide, a man with a thick Bronx accent named Eddie, kept a running narration as they went along, often making the passengers laugh.

The bus turned around at the Stock Exchange and headed back toward where they'd started, near Bryant Park. When it was time to get off the bus, Jacob glanced over at Elka. "You ready for that hotdog now?" The park was across the street, as were several food carts.

"Oh, yes. I'm starving." Elka loved street food.

Jacob's brows pulled in. "This isn't too much walking for you? I could run over there and bring one back."

"No, I can make it. The bus tour was a good idea. Thank you!" Elka pushed her chin up. "I just need to be at the Children's Aid Society by three." She glanced at her watch. There was still some time left.

"Okay, but at least let me help you one more time with those steps." Jacob held out his hand to take her crutches.

It wasn't all bad, having a broken ankle.

After Elka and Jacob got their hotdogs, loaded with sauerkraut, onion sauce, and spicy brown mustard, they sat at a small bistro table together.

Jacob tilted his head to the side. "So, what are you doing at the Children's Aid Society, if you don't mind me asking?"

"I'm going to help some kids with their homework. Today's my first day."

"Oh, really? My mother is a teacher. She retired last year. Do you want to go into teaching?"

"I'm not sure. I guess I'll find out. What grade did your mother teach?" As she asked the question, a big glob of mustard dropped onto Elka's white blouse.

"High school boys." Jacob smiled and shook his head. He didn't seem to notice her clumsiness. "I never got away with anything. She knew everything there was to know ..."

Elka liked the way Jacob spoke of his mother. There seemed to be a lot of love in his family. She dabbed at the mustard with a napkin. It only made it worse. *I can't show up for my first day at the Aid Society with a big stain on my blouse!*

Her watch read, 2:30 p.m. "Jacob, this has been fun, but I should probably get going if I want to be on time. I'll have to go home first and change." She pointed to the mustard stain and shrugged her shoulders.

Jacob's eyes got big. "Oh! Let me get you a cab. That way, you'll have more time."

Considerate, kind, and a whole lot of fun to be with, that was Jacob. Elka was glad she ran into him on the street today. Unfortunately, even with the cab ride home, Elka was late by the time she got to her volunteer job. It wasn't a great way to put her best foot forward.

Mrs. Nadington scowled when she saw Elka, then made a point of checking her watch. "Follow me," she said. "I have someone for you to meet. You're going to be helping Olivia with her homework. She's fourteen."

Elka followed Mrs. Nadington down a long hallway and into a classroom. It was empty, but for one teenage girl with stringy brown hair, huge green eyes, and a face covered in freckles. She was slumped at a desk—Olivia, presumably. The tight jaw, the harsh squint, the crossed arms. Everything about the girl's body language said *I don't want to be here.*

CHAPTER SEVEN

J acob stopped by the grocery on his way home and bought some grapefruits for his friends who were still inside Low library. Now he was standing in front of the building, holding a bag of fruit, trying to figure out how to get it to them. He wasn't alone. There was a crowd of students, many of them also holding bags of food. Some were shouting, others were trying to push past the cordon. It didn't seem to be going well.

The Majority Coalition (aka the jocks), who were opposed to the protests, had taken it upon themselves to try and end the standoff by surrounding the entire library, blocking all doors and windows. They'd made their intentions clear. The idea was to "starve them out." Surprisingly, there were very few cops around at the moment. Where had they gone?

Looking up, Jacob searched the upper floors' open windows, straining for a glimpse of Chase or Colleen. No luck. He heard a kid behind him suggest that they train a bird to take the food into the building. He turned to see who was talking and ascertain whether this was actually a real suggestion. Jacob tried his best to keep a straight face when it became clear the kid wasn't joking. Another student suggested they shoot an arrow at one of the upper-level windows and use it to create a rope and pulley system.

What am I doing out here with these clowns? I should be inside that library, with my friends, fighting against the war ... fighting against racist policies.

Guilt clawed at his conscience. While he'd been enjoying his afternoon, playing tourist with Elka, his friends were inside this building, putting themselves in harm's way, going hungry, putting action to their beliefs. And now he'd lost his chance. There was no way he'd be able to get past the line of muscular jocks surrounding the building. He wasn't seeking a fight, and even if he was, he'd be no match for most of those guys.

Jacob had one more idea. He glanced upward again, this time catching the eye of a girl leaning out a third-floor window. He took a grapefruit out of the bag. "Can you catch it?" The girl nodded and held out her arms. Jacob threw it toward her. She caught it. He grinned and took out another grapefruit.

Monday evening was uneventful. After dinner in the dining hall, Jacob called his mother, studied for a philosophy exam, and went to sleep around eleven. A loud booming sound woke him up a few hours later. He pulled the covers back and ran to the window. He squeezed his eyes shut when he pulled back the curtain. Bright, flashing lights assaulted him. His mind still foggy with sleep, Jacob struggled to make sense of what he was seeing.

A large number of blue-helmeted police officers with shields and billy clubs were moving across the Quadrangle below. They marched in formation toward the library. Behind them, several paddy wagons followed. From a loudspeaker, a voice repeated the same command over and over. "Stay in your rooms."

Jacob dropped the curtain, returning the room to darkness. He stumbled over an open Coke bottle and immediately felt a cold, sticky liquid seep through his socks. Flinging off the soggy sock, he let out an expletive. He switched on his bedside lamp and found a towel to clean up the mess. Now that he was wide awake, it was time to go to the bathroom. Jacob, wearing one sock and his boxers, opened the door to the hallway. At least half the guys on his floor seemed to be out there.

"What's going on?" Jacob asked. "What were those booms?"

"They're arresting the protestors, I think," Michael answered, his voice shaking.

"I was listening over the radio" Sam rubbed the back of his neck, then leaned against the wall. "They're using pepper spray, and they've got dogs with 'em. Hamilton has already surrendered."

Jacob's heart raced, and adrenaline surged through his body. "I'm going out there. Anyone else?"

"Seriously?" Michael shook his head and frowned. "You're crazy. What good would it do to go out there? You don't want to be caught up in that mess, do you?"

"Cover your face and hands with Vaseline before you go out. It will help if you get sprayed," Sam said. He didn't offer to come along.

After Jacob got caught up on the news from the hallway, he returned to his room, determined to make his way to Low library. Colleen was there. Was she safe? He couldn't just stand by and do nothing. Throwing on a pair of jeans, a sweatshirt, tennis shoes, and a hat, Jacob quickly got ready to leave. Was Vaseline really necessary?

The shouts, the barking dogs, and the other sounds coming from outside his window promptly answered that question. Jacob found a jar of the stuff on his dresser and slathered it all over any exposed skin. He grabbed a handkerchief and tied it around his neck. Then he left his room again and headed downstairs.

In Livingston Hall's lobby, Jacob found more students milling about, some ready to go outside, others still in pajamas. The one thing they all wore was an expression of shock, mingled with anxiety. It was three in the morning. It felt more like a nightmare than reality. What were they in for?

Jacob slipped out the front door and braced himself against the cold air. He hustled toward the library, avoiding the well-lit pathways in favor of the lawn's dark, shadowed areas. His shoes were soon soaked through from the dew-covered grass. He didn't want to be seen, and he didn't want to be questioned. The closer he got to the library, the more people filled the area.

"On behalf of the trustees of Columbia and the authority vested in me, disperse immediately," a voice shouted over a megaphone.

The pathway was unavoidable. There was no point in hiding. Now his strategy was to blend in, just one of many in the large crowd. It was unlikely that he would be able to do anything to help his friends, but still, he moved onward, as if pulled by an invisible rope. He could hear singing. It was a song he often heard at protests, "We Shall Not Be Moved."

We're brothers together.
We shall not be moved.
Just like a tree that's standing by the water side.
We shall not be moved.

Walking past a line of cops dressed in combat gear, Jacob tried his best to appear friendly. He made eye contact with one of them and nodded. That greeting was returned with a slight smile, but Jacob averted his eyes after passing several more anger-filled faces. He wasn't here to cause trouble, so why did he feel like he was the enemy?

Now Jacob was back in the same place he'd stood when he threw the grapefruits up to the girl leaning out the window, just a few hours ago. A group of about twenty cops was attempting to get through the front door of the library. They'd successfully opened the door, but it appeared they were now working through multiple barricades between them and the students. The singing seemed to be coming from inside the building. It wouldn't be long until they breached those barricades. His body tensed, like a tightly wound coil, and he reminded himself to be smart. *Don't do anything stupid to get yourself in trouble.*

Jacob's fears continued to mount as green-helmeted officers—the ones who weren't trying to get inside the library — turned their attention to those who were outside. Like a dry tinderbox, it wouldn't take much to ignite an explosion of chaos.

And then it started. Someone lit a garbage can on fire. About a hundred yards away from where Jacob was standing, a cop threw a tear-gas canister toward the students. Running now, away from the cloud of gas, Jacob tried to cover his mouth and nose. He couldn't see where he was going because his eyes were watering and burning. He felt like he was choking. People were screaming. Jacob ran until he reached a grassy area, then he fell on his knees, retching.

Someone pushed a water canteen toward him. "Here, drink."

Jacob took the water and did as he was told. "Thanks," he said, choking out the words. Vision improving now, he took a closer look at the stranger beside him. The guy had a gash on his forehead, and it was bleeding badly." It seems like you're in worse shape than I am." He handed him back the canteen.

"I'll be okay. A cop hit me in the head with his club!" The man seemed to be in a bit of a daze. Shock, probably.

Glancing back at the library now, Jacob saw the police bringing the protestors out of the building. Some were being dragged, and some were carried. Others were more compliant. They were being led to the paddy wagons, hands tied behind their backs.

Jacob watched closely, searching for Colleen. When he saw her, the hair on his arms stood up. Jacob felt the same fierce protectiveness toward Colleen as he did toward his own sisters. She was so small compared to the giant officer who was pushing her forward. Thankfully, she appeared to be uninjured, unlike many of the others. Jacob moved closer. He wanted her to see him and to give her some reassurance.

"Colleen!" Jacob yelled.

She turned toward him and made eye contact. Jacob held up his hand, then shaped his fingers into a "V" sign. It might not feel like it right now, but he had to believe something good would come from the past week. Colleen gave him a weak smile just before boarding the paddy wagon. A few minutes later, she was gone. Now what?

Turning his attention back now to the man with the head injury, Jacob assessed the situation. The guy obviously needed help. "Hey, man, what's your name?"

"Carl." He tried to stand up, but he seemed disoriented and unsteady on his feet.

"Carl, let me help you. Hang onto me." Jacob offered his arm for the man to lean on. Then he scanned the area for somebody who could help. Over by St. Paul's chapel, the lights of an ambulance were flashing. He'd take Carl over there.

As they approached the area, an older man wearing a white collar, identifying him as a chaplain, rushed up to them, carrying a first aid kit. "Are you both injured?" the man asked.

"No, I'm not hurt. This is Carl. He was hit in the head ..." Jacob helped Carl sit down on one of the steps leading up to the chapel. Carl's blood covered his shirt, but other than the lingering effects of the pepper spray, Jacob was fine.

The campus resembled a battlefield. For the next few hours, Jacob worked alongside the chaplain and other volunteers, bandaging wounds, pouring milk over people's faces and eyes, and sending the more seriously injured students away in ambulances. He didn't have time to be angry about all that had happened. There were too many people who needed help right now.

CHAPTER EIGHT

The room could use a good tidying up. Elka scowled at the pile of clothes on the floor, the empty paper coffee cups on the desk, and the overflowing wastebasket. Usually, she didn't let her space get so messy, but everything was more challenging and took more time with a cast on her foot.

The laundry facilities were in the basement of her building. Getting there on crutches while carrying a heavy laundry bag would be her first task of the day. *Five more weeks until the cast comes off. I can make it.*

Elka picked a corduroy skirt off the floor and hung it in her closet, then she switched on the radio, searching for some upbeat music to motivate her for the job ahead. She stopped twisting the dial when she heard Columbia University mentioned. "Over seven hundred arrests were made, and over one hundred students were injured as one thousand police gathered on the campus last night to put an end to the protests," the reporter said.

Hands trembling, she continued to sort through the pile of clothes until she was interrupted by a knock on the door. "Elka, the phone's for you." The voice on the other side sounded like Sarah.

Elka grabbed her crutches, then opened the door. "Thank you, Sarah. Is it Colleen?"

Sarah shook her head. "No, he said his name was Jacob."

By the time she reached the phone at the end of the hallway, Elka's imagination was already in high gear, assuming the worst. She picked up the receiver, hands still shaking, heart pounding. "Hello?"

"Elka, this is Jacob. I'm calling about Colleen."

She'd already guessed that much. "Was she arrested? Was she hurt? I was just listening to the radio."

"She was at the 25th Precinct. But now they're taking her and a bunch of the others to the courthouse for the arraignments. The judge will likely release her on her own recognizance." Jacob paused. "And Elka ... I don't think she's hurt."

Elka felt some tension release from her shoulders. "Did you see her?"

"I saw her last night, right before she got in the paddy wagon. When I heard where they took her, I went down to the station to see if there was anything I could do. But for now, we just have to wait."

Elka let out a deep sigh. "Thank you. So, you were there? What happened?"

"Your sister held out 'till the very end. It was a crazy night. She'll have some stories to tell, I'm sure." He paused. "I want you to know, I'll do everything I can to help her. I did an internship at a law firm last summer. They specialize in this sort of thing …"

Elka's knees weakened. Lawyers? Court? How bad was this going to be? "I appreciate it, Jacob. We're fortunate to have a friend like you."

"It's no big deal. I don't work today, and the school canceled all classes. Are you on duty?"

"It's my day off." Elka noticed Esther, who lived in the room next door, standing in the hallway. She was probably waiting to use the phone.

"If you want, I can come to where you are. From there, we can go together to help your sister."

The laundry and a clean room would have to wait for another day.

Jacob helped Elka out of the cab near the courthouse after paying the driver. He'd refused her money when she'd offered to help with the fare. A large crowd of several hundred people was outside, spilling from the sidewalk and onto Centre Street, forcing traffic to back up. She almost stepped between a reporter and a camera while he was "live" on air.

"Excuse me. Sorry," Elka said, moving out of the way.

Reporters were running all over the place. People were jostling each other to get a better view of the entrance. Between Elka and the building's entrance stood an imposing set of stairs, and at the top, several armed guards stood at the doors, blocking all but a few from entering.

"We must be in the right place." Jacob smiled slightly and nudged Elka with his elbow. His eyes roamed the crowd. He'd kept up a steady stream of banter the whole time they'd been in the cab—an apparent attempt to ease the tension. It was working. Elka returned the smile.

"What do we do now ... just wait?" Elka spotted a group of young people exiting the courthouse, about twenty feet away. One of the guys was wearing a sweatshirt that said Columbia across the front. He was also sporting several deep bruises on his face.

"Yes, when she's released, she'll probably come out that door right there." Jacob pointed toward the man with a bruised face.

Elka felt resigned to the idea that it could be a long while before they saw Colleen, so she moved toward an area of the steps that was less crowded. She had to sit down. A glance at her watch told her it was almost lunchtime. The aroma of soft-baked pretzels from a nearby food cart smelled tantalizing. But now that she was here, Elka didn't want to take her eyes off the door, not even for a second. What if Colleen came out of the building, didn't see her, and then left?

"How much trouble do you think she'll be in? You don't think she'll get kicked out of school, do you? She's a good kid." *And what will our parents do when they find out?*

Jacob shrugged his shoulders. "She's going to be okay. As far as we know, all Colleen was doing was sitting in a building. She wasn't in charge. It's the leaders they'll go after." His tone sounded confident. Did he really feel that way?

A couple of minutes later, Elka spotted Colleen coming out of the front door. "Bugs! Over here!" Her voice cracked with emotion as she stood and waved so her sister could see her.

Colleen's face broke into a smile as she turned toward Elka and Jacob. And very soon after that, she was hugging her sister's neck. "Elka! What happened to your foot?"

Elka shrugged. "A lot can happen in a week—I broke my ankle. I'm fine. Are you okay? I was so worried about you!" She could relax now, knowing Colleen was okay.

"I could use a shower and some sleep, but yeah ... "Colleen shoved her hands in her pockets and bit her bottom lip. "I have a court date next month that I have to come back for. I was charged with second-degree criminal trespassing."

Jacob put a hand on Colleen's shoulder. "That's a misdemeanor. It's not going to ruin your life." He paused. "Colleen, I want to introduce you to a friend of mine. He's a lawyer. He can help you if you want. You've got people on your side."

Colleen brushed a tear off her face and took a deep breath. "Thank you, Jacob."

"It's going to be okay, Colleen." Elka tucked a piece of her sister's hair away from her face. "Now, who wants a pretzel? My treat."

A few minutes later, with pretzels in hand, the three of them left the chaotic scene and found a park bench nearby to sit down. It felt good to reunite with her sister, and Elka was thankful for Jacob's calm, steadying presence. A warm, salty, soft pretzel was the perfect pick-me-up for everyone.

"So, what now?" Jacob asked. "Should I get us a cab?"

Elka needed to be at the Children's Aid Society in a couple of hours, but she also didn't want to leave Colleen, who seemed a little traumatized from her night in jail. "What do you want to do, Colleen?"

Colleen threw a piece of her pretzel to a group of sparrows. "I'd like to go back to my place and sleep."

Fair enough. The poor girl was exhausted. Jacob stood, then offered a hand to Elka to help her up. She took it and smiled. It had been a tough week, but if there was a silver lining, it was her new friend. Or was she beginning to see him as *more* than a friend?

Alone in her room at Morgan Hall, Elka peered from her window toward the Children's Aid Society across the street. Her volunteer shift started in twenty minutes. She wasn't someone to back out of a commitment, and that was the only reason Elka was going back. It seemed she and

Olivia weren't a very good match. The teen had been sullen the entire time she'd been with her yesterday. All of Elka's attempts to get to know the girl had been met with one-word answers or grunts. Maybe this was a bad idea. Was this an experiment gone wrong?

CHAPTER NINE

Jacob dropped his satchel on the floor, kicked his shoes off, and collapsed onto his bed. Sleep was going to feel good. There was still the matter of following through on that promise to help Colleen find a lawyer, but he'd be able to think more clearly after a short nap.

The room was dark when Jacob woke again. Eight-fifteen, according to the clock. It took a moment for Jacob to know if it was evening or morning. He was still wearing his street clothes. That short nap must have stretched into five hours. Unfortunately, the dining hall would be closed for the night. A rumbling stomach reminded Jacob that a pretzel had been the only thing he'd eaten all day.

He reached into his satchel, searching for the Snickers bar stashed away. Pulling out a first aid kit instead, memories from the night before washed over him. The box had been loaned to him by the chaplain at St. Paul's. He'd never gotten the man's name, even though they'd worked side by side into the early morning hours, helping injured students.

The fact that most of those injuries had been inflicted by men whose job it was to "protect and serve" was troubling. Most of the bandages were gone, but Jacob figured returning the kit would be the right thing to do. In any case, he was curious about the man who'd given it to him. First thing, tomorrow morning, he'd search him out.

There, the Snickers bar. Jacob ripped open the wrapper and took a bite. The salty-sweet taste of the chocolate buoyed his spirits. He wanted to call Elka. But was it too soon? Despite the circumstances, he'd enjoyed spending time with her over the last couple of days. He liked her, but she was hard to read. Did she feel the same way about him? Anyhow, he still didn't have a place to stay this summer, so he'd probably be leaving for Seattle soon. What was the point?

Remembering that it was only five o'clock in Seattle, Jacob decided to call his mother instead. She'd likely heard about last night on the news, and she was probably worried. He picked up the phone by his bed and dialed.

She picked up on the first ring. "Hello, this is Ann Lewis."

"Mom, how are you?" Jacob settled back against his pillows.

"Jacob, I'm so glad you called! I've been watching the news. What's going on over there? Are you okay?"

"I'm fine. It got pretty crazy last night on campus, and the cops arrested many students—they were beating people. But I'm okay. Only a few more weeks, and I'm done with school." Or was he already done? It was hard to know. The administration had canceled classes at least through the end of the week.

"Your father and I are looking forward to seeing you. He booked our airline tickets for your graduation ceremony today. We're so proud of you."

I hope there's still going to be a graduation ceremony. Jacob kept that to himself. "It will be good to see you both. I'm still waiting to find out if I'll get the apartment I applied for. I like my job at the Biltmore, and I'd really like to stay here over the summer, if possible." Then, not wanting to hurt his mom's feelings, he added, "I've missed you." It was the truth.

"I've missed you too, honey. You take care now. I'll see you soon."

On Wednesday morning, after leaving a message with the secretary at Maddow, Sinclair, and Associates, Jacob made his way back to St. Paul's Chapel with the first aid kit. The campus was quiet. Cherry blossoms floated through the air, giving the appearance of confetti. When he passed Low Plaza, he took note of how calm it was compared to the week before. The crowds were gone, for now. But a quick scan of one of the posted flyers told Jacob that the conflict was far from over. Students were still organizing further protests.

When Jacob reached the chapel, he paused upon entering. It was a beautiful building with a domed ceiling that could only be described as grand. Light poured in through the arched windows that circled the dome, creating patterns on the floor and walls. The pleasant beeswax scent filled the air and reminded Jacob of his church at home. A feeling of peace settled over him. He should have come here more often over the past few years.

The chapel was empty as far as Jacob could tell. There must be an office for the chaplain. He searched for a sign or something to direct him. Then he heard footsteps behind him.

"Hello, may I help you?"

Jacob turned to see the older gentleman from the other night. "I came to return this. I forgot I still had it in my bag when I went home yesterday morning. I believe it's yours." Jacob offered the first aid kit to the chaplain. "I'm Jacob Lewis."

The man took the kit from Jacob and offered his other hand to shake. "Pastor Simpson. Thanks for your help. I just brewed a fresh pot of coffee in my office. Would you like some?"

"I would. Nice of you to offer." There was something about Pastor Simpson that made Jacob want to get to know him better, even if it meant taking a risk and having to drink a bad cup of java. When it came to the hot brew, Jacob was hard to please, and he didn't like to lower his standards. He loved coffee too much for that.

Pastor Simpson motioned for Jacob to follow him. They walked through the chapel toward a door near the altar. "Come on in, have a seat." He held the door open for Jacob.

Inside the office, the first thing Jacob noticed was the stacks of books on every available surface. It seemed Pastor Simpson was an avid reader. Jacob could smell the coffee, and its rich aroma was promising.

The pastor poured from a carafe into two mugs. "Cream?"

"No, thank you." Jacob sat on a worn old leather chair and took a drink. It was dark and smooth, just the way he liked it. "It's perfect."

Pastor Simpson smiled and settled into the chair opposite Jacob. "So tell me, Jacob, how are you doing this morning?" He tilted his head to the side, waiting for the answer in a way that communicated genuine care.

The pastor's manner of asking the question caught Jacob off guard, and the words that came out his own mouth next surprised even himself. "I guess I'm angry. What I saw the other night was cruelty inflicted upon people. Is that what this country, what this school stands for?" The words came out more forcefully than he'd intended. In a gentler tone, Jacob added, "I'm sorry. I don't mean to sound like that. You're one of the good guys. You were helping."

"I understand the anger, son. The world is a confusing place right now. Fear can make people behave in ugly ways. I don't take sides. All I did was serve the wounded who God brought to this house of worship. Some wounds we can see, others are less visible. It's what I'm here for."

Jacob nodded. "Well, I'm glad to meet you." He put his empty cup on the desk. "I won't take any more of your time. Thank you for the coffee." He stood and offered a handshake.

"I'm happy you stopped by. Come back, anytime." Pastor Simpson stood. "By the way, what are you in school for?"

"Political science. I'd like to go on to law school—just waiting to find out where that will be."

"Ah, well, keep doing the next right thing God brings to you. When you do that, it all works out."

Jacob thought about the pastor's words on his way to midtown later on that day. His friend, Chase, an associate at Maddow Sinclair, had agreed to meet for lunch at the Biltmore Men's Bar. The subway ride gave Jacob time to reflect on what he'd been doing over the past few days.

It had bothered him that he'd missed out on taking a more active role in the protests, but that feeling was fading. Maybe it had all worked out for the best. He was able to help Pastor Simpson at the first aid station, and he was doing his best to assist Colleen and Elka.

What *was* that compulsion he felt toward helping those two? A week ago, he'd barely known either one of them. Was it simply the next right thing? And what about his motives? Was it wrong if helping Colleen allowed for some great excuses to spend more time with her sister? And there was the biggest question. Was pursuing a relationship with Elka the right thing?

Chase was already waiting for Jacob when he arrived. He was seated at the bar, eating a plate of french fries and chatting with the bartender. This was the guy who'd welcomed him on the first day of his internship at Maddow Sinclair last summer. Chase, who, at that time, was fresh out of law school, and Jacob, who was there to assist with research, had hit it off right from the start. They were the only two in the office under forty, and they were both west coast transplants. Chase had a soft spot for underdogs, and Jacob hoped to convince his friend to take on Colleen's case as a favor.

"How's it going?" Jacob slid onto the stool next to his old friend.

Chase wiped the salt and grease from his hands onto a napkin, then slapped Jacob on the shoulder. "I'm good—Susan and I are getting married next month. I wasn't sure where to send the invitation, so I brought it with me." He took an envelope from the inside pocket of his jacket and slid it over to Jacob. "How about you? What's new?"

"Well, I'm sure you've heard what's been going on at Columbia. I have a friend who needs some legal help."

"Oh, yeah?" Chase leaned in to listen.

Those french fries looked appetizing. Jacob signaled to the bartender for a second order. "Second-degree criminal trespassing. She was part of the Low occupation, but the thing is, I don't think she has any money. I just hate to see her get stuck with a court-appointed lawyer. Those guys have so many cases right now, and they can't possibly give each one the attention it deserves."

"My schedule is packed these next few weeks, then Susan and I are taking off for Mexico after the wedding, but I'll meet with her. I'll need your help, though, bro. Give her my card. Tell her to call me."

"Aw, man ... thank you!"

Chase raised his eyebrows. "So tell me, what's her name? And what's your special interest in her well-being?"

"Her name is Colleen Nordeman. I know her from S.D.S. It's nothing like that." Jacob paused and popped a fry in his mouth. His mind went to Elka, and he grinned. "Okay, well, maybe there's something more. She has a sister—"

After saying goodbye to Chase, Jacob wandered over to the lobby in search of Elka. She was stationed at her usual spot behind the front desk. Her dark hair was pulled up into a knot on the top of her head, and her brows were furrowed as she appeared to be concentrating intensely on the ledger she was reading. Gosh, she was cute.

Jacob cleared his throat, making his presence known. She moved her gaze toward him and smiled. He loved the way her eyes lit up and how the corners of her pink lips turned up revealing a dimple on her left cheek. "Hey, I brought you something." Jacob handed her Chase's business card. "Chase Freeman is a friend of mine. He's also a good lawyer, and he agreed to help Colleen pro bono. Please, tell her to give him a call."

CHAPTER TEN

Elka exited the taxi in front of the Children's Aid Society. She'd come straight from work. The fares were really adding up, but what else could she do? The sidewalks of New York were rough for someone on crutches.

Olivia hadn't even bothered to show up yesterday. Elka's patience was growing thin. It wasn't as if she didn't have other things she could be doing with her free time. If Olivia didn't come today, Elka would consider it a sign. Maybe this wasn't the right volunteer job for her. But when she entered the homework room, Olivia was waiting for her.

All right then, let's give this another try.

Elka smiled at Olivia, took off her jacket, and pulled a chair next to her. "Hey, Olivia. How're you doing today?"

Olivia gave a shy smile and straightened her spine. "Hey, Miss Hansen, I'm fine. I like your jacket."

This was an improvement. She hadn't ever seen the girl smile before. "Thanks!" Elka glanced at the garment with a patchwork design. "You know, you can call me Elka."

Olivia dropped the pencil she was holding and turned a deeper gaze on Elka. Her eyes widened, and she bit her bottom lip before speaking. "Elka. Hansen ... I thought so. You're that model, aren't you?"

"I used to model when I was younger, yes. But I don't anymore."

Olivia nodded. "I knew it. Why are you here? You're famous."

Elka smiled. "Used to be. Maybe it's because I missed out on a lot of school when I was your age, and perhaps you're really the one who's here to help me catch me up with what I still need to learn."

"You're lucky. I don't like school." Olivia scowled, seeming more like the girl Elka had first met.

"What is it you don't like about school?"

"I don't have any friends," Olivia said the words in a blunt matter-of-fact tone that broke Elka's heart.

Most of the time, when people recognized Elka, she found it annoying, at best, but she had to admit, her past still brought along some benefits that she didn't mind taking advantage of now and then. If her former life as a model helped her forge a connection with Olivia, then she would be nothing but grateful.

Elka helped Olivia with her Algebra homework for the next hour, but peppered throughout their time together, was an even more valuable sprinkling of shared truths from the heart. Olivia was slowly opening up to Elka, offering her trust.

Olivia asked many questions about what it was like to model and be on the covers of magazines. Elka eventually learned that she could use her answers strategically. For every question she answered, she required two completed equations from Olivia. This way, it didn't take long for Olivia to work through the problems.

A natural camaraderie was developing between tutor and student. Elka suspected that much of the initial coldness Olivia had shown toward her had been a protective mechanism. When it was time to pack up and head home, the initial dread felt upon entering the building that afternoon had been replaced with hope. For the first time since starting volunteering as a tutor, Elka was looking forward to returning.

Outside on the street, Elka waved goodbye to Olivia then hurried toward Morgan Hall. Colleen said she would be in the lobby of her building around five. She'd offered to bring dinner. Elka couldn't wait. A night in with Chinese takeout, comfy clothes, and her sister sounded perfect.

Colleen was waiting, as promised, when Elka arrived. "Okay, Bugs. When you see how messy my room is, don't judge!" Elka raised an eyebrow. "You're not the only one who's had a crazy week. There's laundry everywhere."

"How about I help?" Colleen carried the bag of food while she followed Elka up the stairs. "Why doesn't this place have an elevator yet? Going up and down these stairs on crutches is dangerous. You're lucky you haven't broken any more bones."

"It's an old building. I like a place with history, and I'm okay. I'm getting strong. But I'll take you up on your offer to help with the laundry." Elka took out a key and unlocked her door. "But first, what's for dinner? I'm starving!"

"Chicken chow mein, moo shu pork ... egg rolls." Colleen stuck her nose in the bag and inhaled.

"You can put it on the desk." Elka moved a stack of papers out of the way. "You're the best, sis." Elka moved a pile of clothes off a chair and added them to a heap on the floor. "You can have the chair. I'll just sit on the bed. Let's eat!"

Colleen sat and dug into the carton of chow mein with a pair of chopsticks, sighing with contentment. "You know, we didn't eat half bad during the occupation. People from outside were always bringing us food. Actually, Jacob came by several times with groceries." Colleen narrowed her eyes and pointed a chopstick at Elka. "So what's going on with the two of you, anyway? I saw sparks. That much I know." She grinned.

Elka, who had just burnt the roof of her mouth with an egg roll, ignored the question as she reached for a bottle of Coke, then took a long drink. "I was worried about you. He's been keeping me informed of what's going on with *you*. By the way, have you told Mom and Dad yet?"

"I tried to call when I got arrested, but nobody answered. I only got one call too."

"They're in Florida for the next few weeks."

"Do you think I should tell them?"

"You might not have a choice." Elka reached into her purse, which was hanging on the back of the chair. She took out the business card from the law office that Jacob had given her and handed it to Colleen. "This guy is a friend of Jacob's. He's offered to help you. Give him a call in the morning."

Colleen quirked an eyebrow. "Wow, that's really nice ... okay." She tucked the card away. "Here's what I think. Jacob is a sweet guy and everything, but it wasn't like I knew him that well before all this happened. I'm not going to turn down help, and I'm not complaining, but I think his special interest in helping me might have more to do with the way he feels about you."

Elka brushed some crumbs off her lap and gave her sister a smirk. "I don't know about that."

"Well, he *is* gorgeous, and I wouldn't blame you if you fell for him. I completely support this romance."

"There's no romance. We work together. Besides, he might be moving back to Seattle, where he's from, very soon. There's no point in getting involved if that's the case." Elka grabbed the carton of chow mein. "But yeah ... he is pretty cute." She laughed.

"All right, I'll leave you alone about that, for now, but I want to know more about this cast on your foot. What happened, exactly?"

The sisters finished their dinner, and then Colleen offered to take Elka's clothes downstairs to the laundry room.

"Sis, you're a lifesaver. I didn't even have a clean uniform to wear to work tomorrow."

When Colleen returned to Elka's room after starting the wash, Elka told Colleen about her volunteer work at the Children's Aid Society and Olivia. "I was ready to quit today before I got there. But now, I think I'm all in. She's a good kid."

"Great! That takes some of the pressure off me. Now you'll have another teenage girl to mother," Colleen teased.

"You're not off the hook, girl. You're stuck with me."

It had been a week since Elka's sister had her brief stint in jail and a blessedly uneventful one at that. Only four more weeks to go with the cast. Elka was counting down the days until she could get it removed. Working at the front desk kept the paychecks coming, and for that, she was grateful, but she was anxious to get back to the Palm Court and her job as a hostess. Right now, the lobby was quiet. The phones were silent, and all she needed to do was stand behind the desk and be available to help any customer who approached her.

With less than an hour left on her shift, Elka was also counting down the minutes. She had a date with Jacob. Until now, every place they'd gone together had been the result of an accidental run-in, or it had been all about Colleen. This time it felt different. Intentional. They were planning to go to the theater for an early showing of *2001: A Space Odyssey*, and then he was taking her to dinner.

At three, Anna arrived to take Elka's spot at the front desk. Elka took off her nametag, waved goodbye, and took the elevator up to the employee lounge where Jacob said he'd be waiting.

"Ah, there you are ... you ready?" Jacob's voice sounded flat, and his smile seemed forced. Maybe he was just having a bad day.

"I'm ready. Let's see if this movie lives up to its hype."

Once they were at the theater, settled into their seats with Cokes and popcorn, they had a few minutes to wait until the curtain went up. Jacob cleared his throat. "Have you been to this theater before?" Elka could tell he was trying to fill the awkward silence.

"Yes, a few times." She released a slow, quiet breath of relief when the lights finally went down.

The movie was every bit as good as Elka had imagined it would be, and she was excited to talk about it with Jacob when they got to the restaurant. But Jacob didn't seem so enthusiastic. "Did you like the movie?" Elka asked.

"Yes, I thought it was great. Thanks for coming with me." Jacob seemed to be trying, but his mind was obviously elsewhere.

Elka was about to ask if something was wrong, but then the waiter came to take their order—a cheeseburger and fries for Jacob—a chicken fried steak with mashed potatoes for Elka.

When their server left, Jacob cleared his throat. "I'm sorry I've been so quiet tonight. Today I found out that the manager of the apartment I wanted gave it to someone else. I'm still pretty far down the waiting list for employee housing at the Biltmore. I'm not sure what I'm going to do. I might need to go back to Seattle if nothing else works out."

CHAPTER ELEVEN

Chase's office overlooked Forty-Fifth Street. It was the size of a closet, but it had a window—and a door. This was an improvement. When Jacob interned at the office last summer, Chase had a desk in the hallway. The aroma of freshly baked bagels and coffee filled the small room. Jacob had brought the bagels along with him, knowing how much his friend appreciated them.

"Not too bad, eh?" Chase grinned. "There's a new guy here, so I'm no longer the lowest lawyer on the totem pole."

"You're moving up in the world, friend." Jacob glanced around the space, nodding with approval.

The rest of the office building was empty that Saturday morning, but Chase had volunteered to meet with Colleen outside of his regular billable hours. She'd be here any moment. "I think we can get a plea deal ... maybe some community service, from what she told me on the phone. She's never been in trouble before. We'll see," Chase said.

A knock sounded on the door. *Colleen.* "I wasn't sure if this was the right place. You must be Mr. Freeman." Colleen offered a handshake to Chase. "I'm Colleen Hansen. Thanks, again, for helping me." She smiled in Jacob's direction. "Hey, Jacob."

"No problem. It's nice to meet you. Take a seat." Chase pointed to a small wooden chair near the desk. He sat on the edge of the desk and picked up a file folder. "So ... you're welcome to have a bagel." Chase pushed the bag over to her. "Tell me what happened."

For the next hour, Chase asked questions and listened to Colleen's story while Jacob took notes. Jacob did his best to put his heart into what he was doing, but he was having a difficult time with the role of assistant. Oh, to be on the other side of school and the bar exam, already practicing law. It couldn't come soon enough. He was happy for his friend's success, but the recent letter from N.Y.U. Law, telling him he'd been waitlisted, was a tough pill to swallow.

After Colleen left, Jacob began pulling some files for the case.

Chase poured himself another mug of coffee. "You need more caffeine?" He took a sip, then grimaced. "Yuck, it's lukewarm."

"Ugh ... no thanks." Jacob laughed. "I think everything you need is right here." He pushed the folders over to Chase.

Chase put the folders in his briefcase. "Did you find a place to live yet?"

"Not yet. But there may be no point. I'm only on the waiting list at N.Y.U."

"Ah, that's too bad. I'm sorry, man. There weren't as many people applying to law school when I got in. Now, with so many going to school to avoid the draft, I think there's more competition. Don't give up. Who knows what might happen? Besides, there are good law schools in Seattle too. Right?"

Jacob nodded. Chase was right. But what about Elka? He didn't want to leave New York, just as he was getting to know her. He'd keep trying and praying. Praying always helped.

"Hey, Susan's parents have a cottage in Sag Harbor. We're going out there next weekend. Wanna come?"

Susan Montclaire's family home in Sag Harbor was a couple of hours out of the city. Jacob was going to ride with Chase in his yellow Karmann Ghia convertible, parked on the street in front of Livingston Hall. It was early Saturday morning and already looking like it would be a beautiful, warm spring day.

"First time this year putting the top down!" Chase said as Jacob threw his bag in the back. "Susan is already there. You'll get to meet her parents and her sister, Andrea. They also have a golden retriever named Sam."

Jacob smiled and relaxed. He'd met Susan a few times already, and if her family was anything like her, he was sure he'd like them. It was a shame he wouldn't get to see Elka this weekend. They'd been spending more time together these past few weeks. Though they hadn't discussed anything of the sort, he was starting to think of her as his girlfriend.

"Go ahead and choose some tunes for the trip," Chase said, pointing to the glove box.

Jacob rifled through the eight-tracks until he found what he wanted—Bob Dylan. Then he sat back and enjoyed the ride. One good thing, if he went back to Seattle, he could drive again. Jacob's sister, Claire, had been enjoying the use of his red Mustang ever since he'd left for New York four years ago, and man, did he miss that thing.

When they arrived in Sag Harbor, they drove through a small but quaint downtown area and passed the marina. Jacob smiled when they pulled up to the shingle-style "cottage." The three-story home overlooking the harbor was obviously quite luxurious. The cool breezy air carried the scent of lilacs and seawater.

Jacob stepped out of the car and was immediately greeted with warm, wet dog kisses. "You must be Sam." He scratched the scruff of the dog's neck.

"Chase! You made good time. I didn't expect you here for another hour. How was the drive?" Susan, who'd come out of the house right after Sam, reached up and kissed Chase. Then she turned her attention to Jacob. "It's good to see you again, Jacob. Let me take you inside and introduce you to my family."

Jacob and Chase followed Susan into the house. Inside, her parents came to greet them. Mr. Montclair, a white-haired gentleman with flashing blue eyes, offered a handshake.

Mrs. Montclair, who was an older version of Susan—blonde, thin, and impeccably dressed in a matching pale blue twinset with pearls and neatly pressed slacks—offered her right cheek, *la bise* style. "Hello, Chase. Jacob. Welcome. I hope you like crab chowder. That's what's for lunch."

Just then, a young woman, wearing a black bikini under a sheer black cover-up, strolled into the front room. Her dark glossy hair was piled on top of her head, and even though she'd been sunbathing, she wore thick black eye makeup. "Hey. I'm Andrea." She zeroed in on Jacob, then smiled coyly. "You didn't tell me your friend was so cute, Chase."

Jacob's cheeks burned at hearing the flirtatious compliment. "Thank you for having me this weekend, Mr. and Mrs. Montclair. And yes, I love crab chowder." He could smell it coming from the kitchen.

Mrs. Montclair ignored her daughter's remark and motioned for the housekeeper to take the bags in the entry. "Chase, will you please show Jacob his room? I put him in the one right next to you."

"That's okay, I'll show him," Andrea said.

Jacob noticed the expression on Chase's face. He was obviously trying to hold back a smirk. Chase slapped him on the back, then leaned closer to whisper, "Don't worry. She's harmless, just a flirt. Just know, she's only seventeen."

Nothing to worry about there.

After lunch, Mr. Montclair announced he'd be taking the sailboat out for a few hours. "I have room for three of you. Who wants to come along?"

Mrs. Montclair stood from the table and started gathering dishes to take to the sink. "The girls and I already made plans to go to the shops this afternoon and peek around. Why don't you take Chase and Jacob?" The housekeeper quickly came over and took the dishes out of her hands. "Thank you, Marlene."

"Sounds good to me. Jacob?" Chase stood and kissed Susan on the top of her head. "Have fun, sweetheart."

"Oh, yeah ... I'm in." Jacob smiled. He loved sailing. He also enjoyed seeing his friend so happy. Chase was obviously in love.

Susan pulled Chase's arm as if she wanted to hold onto him and grinned. She stood and kissed him on the lips. "By the way, did you already start forwarding your mail? A few letters came to my place. I brought them here so I could give them to you. They're on the credenza over there." She pointed.

"Yeah, baby." Chase wiggled his eyebrows. "In three more weeks, it will be our apartment!" Chase walked over to the credenza and picked up the stack of letters and rifled through them.

Jacob watched as his friend's smile suddenly dropped. All color left Chase's face as he focused on one of the letters.

"What is it, Chase?" Susan asked.

"It's a draft notice ..."

Everyone in the room stopped what they were doing. Susan started crying. "Can you get out of it?"

"I don't think so. I think I have to go."

"Son ... I suggest you get rid of that letter and enlist straight away. You'll be better off," Mr. Montclair said.

Jacob took a deep breath and tried to think of what to say. He wanted to offer some words of comfort, but what? "I'm sorry, man." It seemed so inadequate.

Susan wiped a tear from her cheek. "How much time do you have?"

"I'm supposed to report to basic training in three weeks."

"Our wedding ..."

"I'm so sorry, babe."

"We can move it up." Mrs. Montclair paced the room, then stopped. "How about this weekend?"

The next day, Jacob was performing best man duties for Chase. Andrea was the maid of honor. The wedding was held on the beach. Other than Marlene, the housekeeper, he was the only non-family member present. It was a sweet and simple ceremony, even though the draft notice left a hint of sadness in the air. It was noticeable in the smiles of everyone at the wedding. Susan was a beautiful bride. Afterward, they celebrated with dinner at The American Hotel.

Jacob offered to drive Susan's Volkswagen Beetle back to the city so she could ride with Chase. They were both good sports, but Jacob knew they were feeling some disappointment and probably fear.

As he approached the city, Jacob thought about why it wasn't a good time to begin a serious relationship with Elka. Nobody had expected the conflict in VietNam to last this long. How much longer would it continue? The heartbreak he'd seen on Susan's face when she'd learned Chase would be going to Nam wasn't something Jacob wanted to witness again. To see a friend in pain like that was awful. He wasn't sure he could bear hurting Elka like that.

Until he had some answers about law school and what was next, maybe the kindest thing to do would be to back off when it came to Elka.

CHAPTER TWELVE

"What happened at the school disciplinary hearing?" Elka leaned her crutches against the wall near the booth and sat next to Colleen.

"I get to stay! And I believe my scholarship is safe too." Colleen poured a generous amount of sugar into her tea and stirred. "Basically, I think what it came down to was that there were too many of us. If Columbia suspended every protestor, they'd be hurting themselves financially. I got off with a *stern* warning." She smiled. "My housing contract in the dorms expires next week, and since I need to save money, I'm moving back home for the summer. I already got a job at the ice cream shop downtown."

"I bet that's a relief. I'm so glad." Elka picked up the menu in front of her, although she already knew what she wanted—a clubhouse sandwich with fries.

"I still might need to come back in July for a court date. My case might be dropped, but if that doesn't happen, do you mind if I stay with you?"

"Of course not." Elka shook her head and tried to hold back a smile. "Bugs ... who knew you'd turn out to be such a troublemaker? Maybe it's a good thing you're getting out of the city for the summer. You can't get into as much trouble in Danbury."

Colleen raised an eyebrow. "I believe it's good trouble, and I'm not sorry. Did you know my lawyer—Jacob's friend, Chase Freeman—has to go to Nam? He's leaving in two weeks."

"Jacob told me. It sounds like Mr. Freeman already has your case pretty much buttoned up, and someone else from his firm will represent you in court if necessary." Elka paused. A waitress came over to the table to take their order. When the woman left, Elka continued. "And I'm just teasing you. I'm proud of you, even if you are making me age prematurely."

Outside the diner, it began to rain. Elka watched through the window as some people on the street brought out colorful umbrellas, and others picked up their pace and hunched their shoulders against the weather.

Colleen set her mug on the table. "Thank you. Now tell me. What's going on with you and Jacob?"

Elka shook her head and sighed. "I really don't know. Maybe I misread him. He's distant toward me. He's still friendly at work, but ever since he came back from his weekend in Sag

Harbor, he doesn't seem to have time for me." She frowned.

The waitress came back with the food. Colleen snatched a french fry off her sister's plate, and Elka rolled her eyes. Colleen always ordered a salad. Why didn't she request her own fries?

"Maybe he's just busy. He graduates next week," Colleen said.

"Maybe." Elka hoped her sister was right. As much as she didn't want to admit it, Elka knew she was already developing feelings for him.

The small diner was getting crowded. The rain seemed to be sending more people inside. Elka spotted David, one of the waiters from the Palm Court, standing near the front door. He seemed to be searching for a table. She waved, and he smiled and waved back.

Colleen watched the exchange. "Do you know that guy? You can ask him to sit with us."

"You don't mind?" Elka glanced back toward David and made a motion with her hand, inviting him over.

David maneuvered his way to the booth, and Elka moved over, making room for him to sit. "Hi, David. You're welcome to join us."

He nodded. "Thank you. Don't mind if I do." He slipped off his rain-soaked jacket, then hung it on a hook near the booth.

"Meet my sister, Colleen," Elka said.

He smiled at Colleen and offered a handshake before sitting down. "When are you coming back to the Palm Court, Elka? You've been missed."

"I get this cast off next week, and then I'll be back."

The waitress came back to take David's order. "That sandwich looks good," he said, pointing to Elka's plate. "I'll take one of those." Then he turned his attention back to her sister. "So, Colleen, tell me about yourself."

She squinted her eyes, and the corner of her mouth turned up into a coy smirk. "Oh, you know, there's not much to tell. I'm a student at Columbia, and I recently spent a night in jail."

The following day, after Elka finished her shift in the lobby, she took the elevator upstairs to the personnel office. She wanted to check the bulletin board and see her spot on the waiting list for employee housing.

Running her finger past the names on the sheet of paper, she found her own. It was still pretty far down the list. Though her room at Morgan Hall was small and stretched her meager budget, it was clean, safe, and conveniently located near the Biltmore. She really couldn't complain. Jacob's name was almost at the top of the list. Only two names were in front of his. That was encouraging. Did he know?

Maybe Jacob was in the employee lounge. Sure enough, she found him there. He was on the couch, watching a Yankees game on television with David. His feet were propped on the coffee table, and a scowl had replaced any smile. Were the Yankees losing?

"Hey, Jacob, David." Elka took a chair next to the couch and glanced at the score. The Yankees were ahead.

"Hey, Elka. Just getting off work?" David stood to leave. "It's time for me to get back. See you around."

"How's it going?" Jacob asked, finally acknowledging her after David left.

"Good. I was just in the personnel office, looking at the housing list. Your name is almost to the top."

Jacob just nodded. Elka was surprised at his response. She'd hoped this would have been welcome news. Was something wrong?

After a long awkward pause, Jacob said, "Thanks for letting me know." Quiet tension hung in the air once again. "David said he had lunch with you today."

"Yes. My sister and I ran into him at Jake's Diner today. We invited him to sit with us because there weren't any more tables."

"Oh—sorry. David didn't mention your sister was there too. I probably sounded petty and jealous just now." Jacob gave an apologetic smile and shook his head.

"Don't worry about it."

Another awkward silence ensued. A little jealousy, however misplaced, gave Elka a glimmer of hope. She'd been starting to doubt whether Jacob had feelings for her. They'd been on a few dates, but they hadn't even kissed. Then this past week had just ... felt off. Maybe they needed to have a conversation about what they were doing. Were they exclusive? She certainly wasn't going to be the one to bring up the topic. Jacob would have to do that himself.

"My parents are going to be here this weekend for my graduation." Jacob stood and turned off the television. The Yankees had won.

That was another thing. Jacob hadn't invited her to his graduation. Would she even get to meet his parents? "Oh. That's wonderful. Have fun." Elka paused. "Well, I'm going to go home now."

Jacob glanced at his watch. "I should probably get to work too."

They took the elevator together downstairs, then said goodbye. When Elka left the Biltmore, she felt as gloomy as the weather outside. The brief glimmer of hope extinguished.

CHAPTER THIRTEEN

J acob approached the front desk, unnoticed, as Elka finished checking his parents in.

"Mr. and Mrs. Lewis, thank you for staying with us here at the Biltmore Hotel. You'll be in suite 305. I hope you enjoy your stay. William will take your luggage and show you to your room."

Jacob, now standing near William, nudged the bellhop. He handed his friend a dollar. "Hey, I don't want you to miss out on your tip. But I'll take it from here. Those people— " He pointed. "They're my parents."

William took the dollar, grinned, and shook his head. "Whatever you say. Thanks, man."

Six months ago, Jacob said goodbye to his family after a brief visit home for Christmas. He'd missed them. Seeing his parents now was the best graduation gift ever—and the expression on their faces when they turned to follow William to their room but found him instead was priceless.

His mother ran to him and gave him a tight hug. "Jacob! How'd you know we were here already? We got in early. I was just going to call you. What a nice surprise to see you."

"I didn't know. I was just arriving for my shift when I saw you." Jacob smiled and kissed his mother on the cheek. Then he turned to shake his father's hand. "Good to see you, Dad. How was the trip?"

Jacob's father affectionately slapped him on the back. "Not bad. They served steak and apple pie on the flight, so I can't complain."

"Ah, yes ... but it couldn't possibly be as good as the steak we serve in the Guard Room." Jacob winked. "If you're up for more steak, come have dinner there tonight. I'll make sure you're seated at one of my tables."

Jacob then remembered Elka was standing there too, watching the whole reunion. He glanced her way and smiled. "So, obviously, you've already met, but Mom, Dad, let me formally introduce you to my good friend, Elka. Elka, these are my parents, Paul and Ann Lewis."

Jacob waited while Elka and his parents exchanged light pleasantries. *Good friend?* That seemed an inadequate way to describe who Elka was to him, but he'd been caught off guard, and he hadn't known what to say. Did he catch a flash of disappointment in Elka's eyes for a brief moment when he said that? Maybe not. Elka wore a professional smile on her face as she handed the room keys to Jacob and said good-bye. Then she turned her attention to the next customer waiting to check into the hotel.

Willian had already loaded the suitcases onto the luggage trolley. Jacob took charge. "I'll show you to your room. Follow me."

"This is a beautiful hotel, Jacob. I'm glad we're finally staying here," his mother said as Jacob led them to the elevators.

Jacob nodded. Even after working at the Biltmore for nearly a year, he still hadn't grown immune to its charms. It had an old-world sense of luxury. The plush oriental rugs, the elevator's gleaming brass doors, rich mahogany paneling throughout the place, and an Italian rooftop garden that converted to an ice-skating rink every winter were some of the features that appealed to Jacob.

"You'll have to check out the Grand Central Art Galleries on the second floor while you're here," Jacob said as he pushed the button in the elevator to the third floor. Then Jacob added a bit of information he thought his parents would appreciate. "Did you know the suite you're staying in is famous?"

"No, why?" asked his mother.

They were at the door to his parent's suite. "Scott and Zelda Fitzgerald stayed here during their honeymoon." Jacob grinned as he put the key in the lock. "They were eventually kicked out because of all their wild partying." He held the door open. "I trust you'll behave better than those two."

His father laughed. "Well, you never know with your mother ..."

Jacob's mom responded with a wink as she threw her hat onto a chair. "Give him a tip, Paul. We have to keep this one happy so he doesn't rat us out."

Jacob laughed. His parents would likely be fast asleep by ten that night, even with the time change from traveling east. He wished he could stay and visit. "If you need anything, let me know, but I need to get to work now."

"Okay." His mother hugged him once more. "We'll come down to your restaurant for dinner in a little while."

"By the way, Son," his father said as Jacob was leaving. "What happened with the apartment search? Are you coming back to Seattle with us this time, or did you find a place?"

"I found a place." Jacob shrugged his shoulders. "I'm on the twenty-sixth floor." He grinned. I moved in yesterday—employee hous-ing."

"Ah, wonderful! Well, we'll talk later. I want to hear more about it."

Jacob was almost out the door when he heard his mother say, "And I want to hear more about your good friend at the front desk, Elka Hansen ..."

He shut the door softly, pretending not to hear those last words from his mother.

Jacob affixed the silky tassel to his graduation hat and tried it on for size. A gold medallion on the tassel, with the number 68, glimmered as he caught his reflection in the full-length mirror. After adjusting his tie one last time, Jacob turned his attention to his mother, who was fussing over his black gown hanging on the back of the closet door.

She made a tut-tutting sound and sighed. "This won't do. There are wrinkles everywhere. Is there a clothes iron here somewhere? I'll fix this."

"It's fine, Mother." Jacob took the gown from the hanger and carefully folded it. "We don't have time. We'll need to leave soon if we want to get to the cathedral on time."

They were in his parent's suite, waiting on his father, who was still getting ready in the bedroom. Jacob walked to the window and gazed at the street below—yellow cabs. He still wasn't sure what he was going to do today. Columbia's commencement would take place at the Cathedral of St. John the Divine. He was relieved it was still happening, despite the canceled classes and the turmoil from the past few weeks.

There was also a separate counter-commencement at Low Plaza. A plan was in place for some of the students to get up and walk out in protest. Many of them were angry with the administration for their poor handling of the protests. He was one of them. To go to the school-sanctioned commencement or the other one—that was the question. If his parents hadn't traveled all the way across the country to be here, it would be an easy choice.

"Everyone ready?" His dad walked out of the bedroom, holding a small box in his hands. "Before we go, I have something for you, Jacob."

"Thank you." Jacob opened the box and smiled when he found a pair of gold cufflinks with the letter *L* engraved into them. "These are incredible."

"Here, let me help you with those," his mother said.

"The cufflinks were your great grandfather's. They were given to him by Marshall Field on his wedding day."

"Marshall Field, from the department store?" Jacob was impressed.

"Yes, as the story goes, Mr. Field was something of a mentor to him back in the day." Jacob's father gave him a pat on the back. "I'm proud of you, Son."

After the ceremony, Jacob found his parents on the street outside the cathedral. They were both wearing big smiles. He'd made the right choice in not walking out. Today was as much for them as it was for him.

"Okay, graduate." Jacob's father gave him an affectionate slap on the shoulder. "I made some reservations for us at the Rainbow Room. We should probably get going."

"Wait, I need to get some pictures first!" His mother waved her camera. "Jacob, stand with your father over there."

Jacob obliged his mother and stood for countless pictures for the next ten minutes. When they finally got in the cab to go to dinner, his cheeks were aching from smiling so long.

The Rainbow Room was atop Rockefeller Center. Jacob was sure there was no better view of the city in all of Manhattan. Dusk was setting in. Like stars, the city's lights were emerging, a few at a time. The Empire State Building was framed by the window they were seated at. He was happy to be here with his parents, but Jacob couldn't help but think, this was a place he'd love to bring Elka.

After they ordered their meal, his father took a sip of wine, shifted back in his seat, and cleared his throat. So far, the conversations he'd had with his parents during their time here had been casual. He knew his father had been waiting for the right time to bring up more serious matters, like what was next for Jacob.

"Have you made a decision yet about law school, Son?"

"Seattle University accepted me, and I'm on the waiting list at N.Y.U." Jacob took a bread roll out of the basket in front of him.

"S.U. is a good school, and we'd love to have you closer to home. Where's the hesitation coming from? You'll need to give them an answer soon, or they'll give your spot to someone else."

"I know. I will. You're right. I should be happy to go to Seattle University." Jacob hesitated.

"It's just, the timing of this has been awful. I met someone—"

Jacob's mother placed her hand on top of his. "The girl at the front desk you introduced us to?"

How did she know? "Yes."

His mother smiled. "She's a beautiful girl. Why does she seem so familiar?"

"She used to model. That's probably why."

"Ah, yes ... I thought so." Jacob's mother shook out her napkin and placed it in her lap. "Elka ... Hansen ... that's right! I saw her on several of your sisters' *Seventeen* magazine covers."

The waiter set three mouthwatering plates of ravioli in front of each one of them.

Jacob's father cleared his throat again when the waiter left. "So are you two dating? Are you serious?"

"Not exactly. "Jacob took a bite of ravioli. "I mean, we've been on a few dates, but with everything up in the air ... Until a couple of days ago, I didn't even know if I'd have a place to live this summer."

"Does she know how you feel?" His mother furrowed her brow. "Why didn't you invite her to your commencement?" Straight to the point, as always.

"I ... I don't know." Why didn't he invite her? Maybe he should have. Did he hurt Elka's feelings by not asking her to come today? As he thought about his interactions with her over the past few days, he got a sour taste in his mouth. He'd been a dolt.

"Well, it seems to me you don't have long to figure these things out, Son. Time is not on your side. Use the days you have left wisely."

Was it too late?

CHAPTER FOURTEEN

Elka felt graceful, buoyant, and free in the water. Her arms and legs moved in a meditative rhythm as she completed her twentieth lap that morning. The employee pool at the top of the Biltmore was where she'd broken her ankle, and now it was where she'd work on healing it.

After the doctor removed her cast, she'd gasped at the shriveled skin underneath. After six weeks in the plaster, her right leg muscles were noticeably smaller than her left.

"Don't worry. It will look normal in no time," he'd told her. "If you have access to a pool, I suggest swimming to regain your strength."

Nobody else was here at the moment, and Elka was enjoying her solitude. It gave her time to think. Her sister had gone back to Connecticut for the summer. The court had accepted a plea on the trespassing charges. Colleen would fulfill some required community service in the fall, but thankfully, the worst of it was over. They both owed a debt of gratitude to Jacob, who'd gone above and beyond in helping to sort out her sister's legal issues.

She'd misconstrued Jacob's kindness. Elka felt like a fool. It was a mistake she didn't intend to make again. He'd introduced her to his parents the other afternoon merely because she'd been standing right there. They seemed nice—though it was clear they were two people who'd never heard a single mention about her from their son.

Jacob didn't see her as girlfriend material. *Good friend*, that was the term he'd used. Well, she could do that. She could be his friend. But from now on, she'd guard her heart.

Intentionally turning her thoughts away from Jacob now, Elka did her best to regain the sense of peace she'd felt before her mind had taken a detour to that sad place. She paid attention to the soft, lapping sound of the water as her body sliced through the coolness. It soothed her.

Elka reached the end of the lane and pushed herself out of the water and onto the deck. She sat for a moment and waited until her breathing slowed down. It had been a good workout. She was just reaching for her towel, about to get out of the pool, when the sound of a door opening and closing broke the silence.

She stayed put, keeping her feet in the water. She felt conscientious about the appearance of her shriveled right leg. A glance to see who would be joining her revealed Jacob. He waved and came over to where she was sitting. His perfectly athletic and tanned torso was shirtless, and he carried a towel over his shoulder.

Elka averted her eyes. He was too handsome. These were not friend thoughts. She quickly pushed them away. Jacob smiled, and her heart skipped a beat.

"You got the cast off!"

The water hid nothing, and she cringed inside as his eyes moved to her right leg. "Yeah, I'm going back to working in the Palm Court this afternoon. Thanks for all your help over the past few weeks." She wrapped her towel around her shoulders. "Did your parents have a good visit?"

"Yes, I think so. My mother recognized you from your magazine covers. She kept asking about you." Jacob sat next to her and put his feet in the water. "Hey, would you be interested in going out to Coney Island with me next Monday? You still have Mondays off, right? It could be a fun way to celebrate you getting rid of those crutches."

Coney Island. With Jacob. Was this a friend thing or a date? Would saying yes go against her newfound resolve to think of Jacob only as a friend? She stalled in answering by getting up and putting on her cover-up. She couldn't think of any excuse why she should say no. After this Thursday, her tutoring job with Olivia would be on pause for the summer. "Okay. We'll take the subway?" The words came out before she could take them back.

"Yes, it will take about an hour to get there." Jacob put on his swim goggles. "It's a date. How does ten sound? I can meet you in the lobby of your building."

A date. *Oy vey*. Maybe she should try to get out of this before it was too late. Only ... Elka didn't want to get out of it. "Sounds good."

Jacob jumped in the water. Did he have any idea how hard it was to say no to him? How stupidly charming he was?

And ... was she more annoyed with him or herself?

Olivia's junior high school was a quick walk from the Biltmore. Elka carried a small gift box and a bouquet of daisies as she approached the large brick building with red doors. She usually worked on Thursdays, but today was a special day. Olivia had invited her to attend her eighth-grade graduation ceremony.

Elka felt honored to have been included in Olivia's milestone moment. The invitation was a sweet gesture, and it had helped to ease some of the disappointment she'd felt over being excluded from Jacob's commencement ceremony.

Though she'd signed up on a whim, owing in large part to her broken ankle and a different work schedule, volunteering at the Children's Aid Society had been more rewarding than Elka had expected. She'd realized an excellent way to take her mind off her problems was to help someone else with theirs. It had been gratifying to see Olivia's confidence grow over the past six weeks. The girl had gone from a failing grade in Algebra to a solid B. Not bad. Pouring some extra love and attention into a teen's life wasn't difficult. Elka enjoyed the work. She didn't even need to be a math whiz to be a decent tutor, just proficient and patient.

She found the big red doors to the school entrance where a small crowd of parents and grandparents were congregating outside the building. Feeling a little bit like a proud parent herself, Elka followed people inside and down a long hallway toward the gymnasium.

"Elka, over here!" Olivia stood and excitedly waved from the bleachers where she sat with her class.

Elka smiled, waved back, and found a seat on a folding metal chair with the parents. The ceremony was about to begin. A tall lady with cropped gray hair stood at the podium and introduced herself as Mrs. May, the school principal. She had some nice things to say about all the students. Then the school choir sang a few songs. The music was followed by the handing out of awards.

Olivia received a good citizenship award, and Elka clapped just as any proud parent would. Were Olivia's parents here? Elka glanced across the crowd, seeking out anyone with a resemblance. Olivia never talked about them. Elka suspected that she and her student shared the fact that they both had absentee parents.

When the short ceremony had concluded, Mrs. May invited the parents to mingle in the gym. Platters piled with an assortment of cookies and punch bowls filled with a red bubbly drink sat on a long table. Elka took a chocolate chip cookie while she waited for Olivia to make her way over.

Mrs. Nadington, the director of the Children's Aid Society, was getting a cookie too.

"Hello, Elka ... good to see you here." The woman had warmed considerably toward Elka over the past few weeks.

"Mrs. Nadington. How are you?"

"I'm good, thank you. You and Olivia really worked well together." The director scooped a ladle of punch into a Styrofoam cup. "I hope you'll consider coming back in the fall when school starts again."

"I'd like that, as long my work schedule allows. I'll let you know."

The two of them made small talk until Olivia joined them.

"Congratulations, Olivia." Mrs. Nadington smiled and offered a handshake, then excused herself to greet some of the other students she was there to see.

"I brought you something." Elka handed the flowers and the gift box to Olivia.

"Thank you. I'm glad you came." Olivia smiled as she opened the box and discovered the tube of Revlon shimmer pink lipstick. She immediately put some on and rubbed her lips together.

"You're a high schooler now, so I thought it was only fitting. I started wearing lipstick when I was your age." Elka paused. "Will your mother approve?" She glanced around the room. "Is she here? I was hoping to meet her."

"She won't care—and no, she's not here." Olivia looked down at her feet, offering no other explanation. Elka put her hand on the girl's shoulder in understanding.

"So what are your plans for the summer?" Elka wiped a cookie crumb off her blouse. She ignored the stares coming from a group of young girls near the doors. "Will I see you again in the fall?"

"I'm going to summer camp upstate. But after that, I'm moving to New Jersey. Can I write to you?" Olivia frowned, then opened her satchel and started searching for something.

Elka pulled a pen and paper from her purse and wrote her address on it. "I don't know how much longer I'll be at this address either, but I would love it if you wrote to me. And, of course, I'll write back." She handed the paper to the teenager.

Olivia put the paper in her satchel and nodded toward the door. "Those girls over there recognize you. They didn't believe me when I told them we were friends."

Friends. Elka loved that Olivia thought of her as more than an acquaintance. She felt the same way. "I'm happy we're friends, Olivia." She smiled. "I need to go back to work. Thank you for inviting me today."

As Elka walked back to the Biltmore, she had an extra spring in her step. Olivia's words had given her hope. Maybe Mrs. Nadington would be able to match her with another teenage girl for tutoring in the fall.

On her way to work, Elka stopped at the newsstand on the corner of Fifth Avenue and Forty-Fifth to pick up breath mints. A startling headline caught her attention. Robert F. Kennedy was dead—shot by an assassin.

Hands shaking, Elka handed a dime to the proprietor to pay for her mints. She averted her eyes from the newspapers, as if not knowing would make it unreal. Martin Luther King Jr. in April and now the Attorney General? Would there be riots again? Thank God, Colleen was out of the city.

CHAPTER FIFTEEN

In the four years he'd lived in Manhattan, Jacob had rarely ventured over to Brooklyn. On the ride out, Elka revealed she'd never been to an amusement park before. Funny how they'd both missed out on this place until now. It was fun seeing Elka's joyful reactions to all that Coney Island had to offer. Her eyes lit up with excitement.

Though it was still early in June, the heat radiating from the boardwalk made the sparkling blue water at Brighton Beach a welcoming sight. Loud tinny music, combined with the clanking chains from the rides, screams, laughter, and the pinging of pinball machines, made hearing each other nearly impossible. But with Elka, there didn't seem to be a need to fill every moment with words. For the most part, they were at ease together.

One uncomfortable moment occurred when they exited the subway. Jacob tried to reach out and hold Elka's hand, but she avoided him. She'd tried to appear nonchalant, as if there was a sudden need to fasten her hair into a ponytail, but the message had been clear. She was holding Jacob at arm's length.

Of course, he was probably responsible for the change in Elka's behavior toward him. She was friendly, while at the same time keeping her distance. He'd done the same thing to her after returning from Sag Harbor.

They passed an ice cream shop. The irresistible aroma of freshly made waffle cones wafted from the doorway, and Jacob stopped. "Would you like some ice cream?"

"Definitely!" Elka grinned. When they reached the counter, she pulled out her coin purse to pay. She'd been trying to pay for everything today.

Jacob refused the money. "My treat."

After they had their cones, they wandered back outside and found a bench overlooking the beach. The area was already getting crowded. "After this, do you want to go down to the water?"

"Sounds good to me." Jacob pointed toward the marquee that read, *Luna Park*. "My grandpa used to tell me about a place called Luna Park in Seattle. He used to go there when he was young. It was named after this one."

Elka gazed into the distance. "That's interesting. Tell me more about Seattle. What's it like?" She was a good listener.

As Jacob told her about his hometown, he realized that he missed it in many ways. "So, how is it that you've managed to make it into your twenties without ever visiting an amusement park?"

Her face took on a more serious expression. "When I moved to New York, it was for work, and I've been working ever since. There hasn't been a lot of time for leisure pursuits. Modeling didn't allow for much of a childhood. I spent a lot of time with adults on sets."

"What was your life like before you moved to New York? In Pennsylvania?"

"We were poor. I mostly took care of my sister. She's five years younger than me. When I started getting work as a model, my parents didn't have to work as much. Our lifestyle improved. We got to move to New York. I was proud of all that, but it was also a lot of pressure, being the main breadwinner and all."

Elka twisted a silver ring on her finger and paused. "When I turned eighteen, I had a ... an unfortunate experience with a photographer. He was a real creep, and he took advantage of me. I'd already started losing interest in the work, but after that, I knew I couldn't continue. That caused some problems with my parents. They didn't want me to quit modeling—but I wanted to go to college. I wanted to move on. I felt used, and I was angry. Soon after all that, they moved to Connecticut, but I stayed here."

She shrugged her shoulders. "I don't have the money to pay for college yet, but I'm working on it. And I'm still trying to figure out what I want to do with my life. I still feel responsible for my sister. She's so young. I don't want her to feel alone—or unprotected—in this big city." Elka stopped and laughed when she saw her ice cream cone had melted and dripped all over her bare leg. "I guess I'm talking too much."

Jacob smiled and handed her a napkin. "Not at all. Thank you. I'm glad you told me." He'd be more careful with Elka's feelings going forward. He wanted to protect her.

"You know, I think I owe you an apology," he said. "I got a little spooked when Chase received his draft card while I was in Sag Harbor. Seeing how it didn't just affect him, but also Susan, made me think of you. I care about you a lot. The idea of starting a relationship at a time like this is scary. But I didn't explain any of that. I just backed off."

He took off his sunglasses. "I have no idea what's going on with my future right now, but I do know I want you to be part of it. If you're willing to be okay with some uncertainty and take a risk on me, I would love it if you'd consider being my girlfriend."

Jacob could feel his heart beating in his chest. He held his breath as he waited for Elka to reply. She took his hand and traced her finger over his thumb. Her skin was so soft.

"Yes." Elka grinned. "I'd like that." She paused. "What happened to Robert Kennedy last week got me thinking. Everything can change in an instant. I'd rather live each day to the fullest. Nobody's future is guaranteed."

It was as if time stopped right there, and no one else existed. Jacob reached over to Elka and tucked a loose strand of hair behind her ear. Her hair smelled clean and citrusy. His fingers moved to trace the skin along her cheek. She looked up at him, her dark eyes full of trust.

Adrenaline pumping, he moved closer, bringing his lips toward hers. She met him halfway and brought her hand to the back of his neck. The taste of strawberry and vanilla from her lips lingered even after he pulled away. Her kiss invaded all his senses. The rest of the day was nothing but a happy blur.

On Monday night, Jacob returned to his room at the Biltmore feeling euphoric. With one hand, he carried a plastic bag with the goldfish Elka had won for him at the arcade. In the other—a giant pickle jar sloshing with water, which he'd picked up from the Guard Room's kitchen on his way upstairs. It would have to suffice as a temporary home. The fish also needed a name. Penny? It was the same color. That would work.

After getting Penny situated in her new home—the pickle jar on top of his dresser—Jacob rifled through the stack of unopened mail waiting for his attention. The return address on one particular envelope caught his attention, immediately giving him the feeling of being punched in the stomach. *Selective Service.* He opened it, then unfolded the contents and read the first line at the top.

Order to report for induction.

CHAPTER SIXTEEN

The change in the clientele at the Palm Court was noticeable. Most of the regulars had left for their summer homes outside the city. The restaurant was still busy, however, as the tourists had come in their place.

Elka stood at her podium near the large clock as a group of five middle-aged women, who did not appear to be tourists, approached. They must be Peterson, party of five. Elka gave her brightest smile, even though she didn't feel like it. It was her job, and her mood didn't matter. She would be professional, as always.

Before her shift started, she'd gone upstairs and spoken with Jacob. He'd told her he'd accepted a spot in the law school at Seattle University. He'd be going back to Washington in the fall. It was law school or Viet Nam. There wasn't any more time left to wait and see if he could still get into NYU's law school. She understood, but it didn't make his decision any easier for her. Would a long-distance relationship survive? Would he even want that?

As the women came closer, Elka saw Mrs. Nadington among them.

"Hello, dear. So this is where you work ..." The director from the Children's Aid Society offered Elka her cheek for an air kiss. Then she whispered into Elka's ear, "It was serendipitous that I came in today. There's something I need to tell you. Not now, but I'll come back and speak to you at a more suitable time.'

Elka nodded, acknowledging she'd heard. Then took some menus and led the ladies to their table. She was curious about what Mrs. Nadington needed to tell her. The tone of the message had seemed rather serious, although this wasn't altogether out of character for the woman. Did she have bad news?

With frazzled nerves, Elka waited impatiently for the next hour. Her imagination was getting the best of her. It was simply wrong to string someone along that way. If a person had something to say, they should just come out with it. The lunch rush slowed down, so Elka tried to keep herself busy by folding cloth napkins into swans.

Finally, Mrs. Nadington and her friends finished their meal and got up from their table. When they all walked toward the door, Elka wondered if Mrs. Nadington had forgotten about her. But she waved goodbye to her friends, then turned on her heel and came back toward the Palm Court.

"Elka … Olivia's mother came to see me," she said, this time getting straight to the point. "Olivia went missing about a week ago. Her mother thinks she ran away. I thought you would want to know. If she shared anything with you that might give us a clue to her whereabouts, we need to know."

Elka's skin prickled. Her mouth felt dry. "She said she was going to summer camp, and that she was moving. She promised to write, but I haven't heard anything from her."

"According to her mother, she never arrived at camp. She disappeared the night before she was supposed to leave. If you do hear from her, please let me know. Unfortunately, this happens all too often. There are a lot of places for runaways to hide in this city." Mrs. Nadington's face softened, and she placed her hand on Elka's shoulder. "I'm sorry for the disappointing news."

"I'm glad you told me. I want to help. She never shared much with me about her situation at home. If I hear anything, I'll be in touch."

Elka said goodbye to Mrs. Nadington, then headed toward the elevator. Her shift was over. She wanted to find Olivia, but where should she even start to search? The thought of her young friend, so vulnerable and on her own was almost more than she could bear. And what if she hadn't run away at all? What if she'd been kidnapped?

After changing out of her work clothes in the locker room, Elka decided to go for a walk. She didn't expect to find Olivia, but maybe she could ask around and speak to some of the school kids.

For the next four hours, Elka wandered around midtown, paying special attention to places where teens hung out. It all felt a little pointless. If Olivia didn't want to be found, there was probably little chance of finding her. But Elka had to try.

The Horn and Hardart automat near the hotel had become a favorite meeting place for Elka and Jacob, now that he lived at the Biltmore. They often met there for breakfast, the rare time when neither one was on duty at the hotel.

Elka saw Mr. Sawyer, the retired policeman, sitting alone by the window. "Fancy meeting you here." She smiled and pulled up a chair next to him, not even bothering to ask if it was okay. They were past such formalities now. They'd shared several meals since that first one when she'd been on crutches. Jacob joined them, then arranged their bagels and coffees on the table.

"Elka, Jacob. Good to see you." Mr. Sawyer folded the newspaper he'd been reading and put it to the side. "What's new since I saw you last?"

Elka spread cream cheese on her bagel. "Not much." She sighed. "Well, actually, you know how I was tutoring a girl at the Children's Aid Society? She's gone missing. Most likely, she ran away."

Mr. Sawyer nodded sympathetically then took a sip of coffee. "Do you think she's still in the city?"

"I really don't know."

"How old is she?"

"She's only fourteen."

Jacob put his hand on Elka's in a comforting gesture. Over the past week, she'd started calling her searches for Olivia her *walkabouts*. When he wasn't at work, Jacob often came along.

Mr. Sawyer's expression was thoughtful. "There are a lot of runaways in the East Village. It's a dangerous situation, especially for a girl her age. Most of the time, the kids who run away find surrogate families made up of other *troubled* teens, which helps them blend in and harder to find. They think they've found independence, but there's often a heavy price pay."

Elka sat back and rubbed her neck. Mr. Sawyer's unvarnished words were hard to swallow, but she knew he was telling the truth. "Is there anything I can do?"

"I've been retired for a while now, but I still have a few friends on the force. I'll do some asking around. Her parents have already filed a report?"

"Yes, they did … and thank you." Elka fiddled with the napkin in her hand. "I think I'll go explore the East Village after work tonight." Elka took a sip of coffee. She'd go now, but she needed to be at the Biltmore in an hour.

"Elka, don't go wandering around by yourself. I'd be happy to go with you." Mr. Sawyer reached into his pocket and pulled out a pen. He scribbled a phone number on a napkin and passed it across the table. "I live close by. Just give me a call if you need some company on your walk."

Jacob leaned forward in his chair. "He's right, Elka. I don't get off until eleven tonight. I can go with you after that, but if you don't want to wait, please, take Mr. Sawyer up on his offer." He gave an approving nod toward the former policeman. "Thank you. You're a good man."

Mr. Sawyer cleared his throat, seemingly embarrassed by the compliment. Then he focused his gaze on Elka. "If you do find this girl, then what will you do? Often, when I was on the force, we'd pick up a runaway, take them back to their folks, and they'd leave home again as soon as they got the chance."

Elka nodded, then stared at the checkered floor as she thought for a moment. "I guess I would want to talk to her and make sure she's okay." She knew her answer was inadequate. Olivia ran away for a reason. What if she didn't want to come back?

"I'm not trying to discourage you. I hope you find her." Mr. Sawyer offered a weak smile. Then he finished his breakfast. Standing from the table, he put his hat on. "I'll see you around. And Elka, I mean what I said. Call me anytime. I'll help you search for your friend."

After Mr. Sawyer left, Elka reached over and squeezed Jacob's hand. "I'm sorry. Here you are, with only a few weeks left in the city, and you're spending all your free time helping me find a lost girl."

Jacob moved his chair closer to her. His eyes crinkled at the edges as he studied her face. "It seems to me you've got a soft spot in your heart for—how shall I say it—troubled youth. First, your sister, and now Olivia. I love that about you."

Elka furrowed her brow. She wasn't sure she'd describe her sister as troubled. Would she? "Well, I don't know about that." She laughed. "Maybe I'm just one of those people who's drawn to drama. And I would say, if anyone has a soft heart, it's you."

Jacob reached out and softly brushed her cheek. "I think you have something to do with that."

Elka felt her skin flush. Jacob had a way of doing that to her. She still got butterflies in her stomach when he looked at her in that sweet way of his—like he saw the best in her—not the superficial, outward appearance, but the deeper and real side of her. It made her want to try to live up to his high opinion of her. Even if she wasn't sure she could.

CHAPTER SEVENTEEN

It had been a gloomy day. It sure didn't feel like the Fourth of July. The city was quiet. Jacob didn't get to see Elka because she had gone to see her family in Connecticut. Many people had left the city to observe the occasion elsewhere—that is, the people who felt like celebrating.

Jacob wasn't one of them, which was why he had no problem with working tonight. He could try to pretend it was just any other day. However, it would be nice if there were a few more customers. It was a slow night—too quiet. The room felt like all the energy had been sucked out of it. Jacob glanced at his watch. Eight o'clock, only thirty minutes had passed since the last time he'd checked. A steak restaurant in midtown wasn't generally the place to be on Independence Day.

All Jacob could think about was the never-ending, unjust war that was causing nothing but death and destruction—and the leaders, like Robert Kennedy and Martin Luther King Jr, who dared to speak against it—killed. Jacob loved his country. But today felt more solemn than celebratory.

Jacob was one of the lucky ones. Not every guy his age could get out of the war. A deferment for law school was a privilege not afforded to most. His upcoming move back to Seattle—when all he wanted was to stay in New York with Elka—was making him feel miserable.

He'd received mail from NYU Law today, telling him he was no longer on the waiting list. There was an open spot for him. But he'd already plunked down all the money he had for the first quarter's tuition at Seattle University. If not for the terrible timing of that summons from the Selective Service, he wouldn't have needed to rush his decision regarding law school. How did the saying go? *A day late and a dollar short.* That was it. Well, there was nothing more to do. He'd just need to deal with it.

The group of four at table nine appeared to be finished with their meal. Jacob kept a careful eye on his customers from the corridor between the dining room and the kitchen. Waiters caught a breath there when they had a few minutes to spare. Tonight, there was plenty of time. He prepared the check and slid it into a leather folder.

Randy, another waiter, nudged Jacob. "You got an extra pen I could borrow? My last customer walked off with the only one I had left."

Jacob took a pen from the inside of his suit jacket and handed it to his coworker.

"Thanks, man. Hey, some of us are going to catch a show in the village tonight after work. Some comedian named Louis Fey. Want to come?"

Why not?

Confident self-expression and a counter-cultural ethos made Greenwich Village feel like another world away from midtown, even though it was only a subway stop away. Jacob liked it here, even if it was a little rough around the edges.

Jacob, Randy, Chuck, and Pete entered a dark, smoke-filled comedy club called The Black Box a little after midnight—just in time for the main event. The four guys found a spot to stand by the bar since the tables were all taken. Maybe this comic, Louis Fey, really was as funny as Pete claimed. He'd certainly pulled in a crowd. The room held an aroma of piney, slightly skunky grass mixed with beer and sweat. Jacob felt like a square. His gray stovepipe pants and black turtleneck sweater didn't exactly fit in with the hippie aesthetic.

"First round on me," Randy said. Then he pushed his way forward through the crowd to make an order at the bar.

"Are you guys looking for a place to sit? You can join us over there."

Jacob turned to see a girl with a teased blonde bouffant pointing toward a table in the front of the room, near the stage. Two of her friends waved them over from where they were sitting.

"I'm Jewel." Her invitation had included all of them, but her gaze focused on Chuck. He was always popular with the ladies.

Jacob stayed behind to help Randy carry the beers to the table. He took two of the glasses. "Hey, so while you were ordering, some girls invited us to sit with them at their table over there."

Randy and Jacob joined the group at the table near the stage just as Louis Fey came out. His stand-up routine ran the gamut, from jokes about growing up in suburbia to making fun of politicians. It felt good to laugh, and Jacob was glad he came. He'd been in a bad mood all day, but he was feeling better.

After Louis Fey finished his set, Jacob checked his watch. There were more comedians on the docket, but it was already close to 1:00

a.m. Elka would be coming back on the train in the morning, and she'd asked to meet-up before their shifts started at work. They were going to take some bagels and coffee to the park. If he got his act together, maybe he could even stop and pick up some flowers. That would mean waking up early, so staying out too late was probably a bad idea.

But the guys were having fun—especially Chuck, who had his arms around Jewel. She was sitting on his lap, laughing at something he was whispering in her ear. Jacob didn't want to spoil the party. He'd leave them to it.

"Thanks for inviting me along. I've got an early morning tomorrow, so I'm going to head out." Jacob opened his wallet, put a dollar on the table for his share of the drinks, and then waved goodbye.

Exiting the stairwell from the club onto the street, Jacob saw a group of about eight scruffy youths nearby, smoking joints. Over the past few weeks, he'd been on plenty of walkabouts with Elka, always on the lookout for Olivia, a four-teen-year-old girl he'd never met. Jacob only had a rough description of her—five foot five, shoul-der-length straight brown hair, blue eyes, lots of freckles. Out of habit, he glanced at the kids' faces as he walked past, wondering if one of the girls might be Olivia.

Sitting on an upturned crate was a girl who could fit the description. She seemed younger than the rest of the kids in the group. Jacob noted that she was wearing a purple miniskirt and a colorful patchwork coat.

One of the guys narrowed his eyes toward him. "What are you looking at?" His voice sounded menacing.

Jacob ignored the question and kept on his path toward the subway, but he could hear footsteps behind him. A lone yellow cab came around the corner. Jacob moved toward the curb and raised his arm, but the driver switched the off-duty light on and drove by. Continuing toward the subway station at a quicker pace now, Jacob listened as the sound of the footsteps behind him kept pace with his. This continued even as he turned onto Christopher then crossed the street. They were definitely following him.

When he reached the stairs to go down into the subway, Jacob heard the same menacing voice that had spoken to him outside the comedy club. "Stop right there."

An ominous feeling came over Jacob, but he stopped anyway. Three guys surrounded him. One of them pulled up the edge of his shirt to show a knife tucked in his waistband. "What do you have on you?"

"Just my wallet." There was nothing more than a couple of dollars in there. Nothing worth risking his life for.

"Hand it over."

Jacob reached into his back pocket and gave it to the guy. Would they let him go now? Just then, an ambulance came by, lights flashing, siren on. Seeing this momentary distraction as his opportunity to get away, Jacob took off and ran down the stairs toward the turnstiles.

He still had a subway token in his front pocket. His hands fumbled with it while trying to push it in the slot. Finally, he heard the click of the coin dropping. Jacob pushed forward, then he ran toward the platform, hoping he wouldn't be alone. One man was sitting on a bench, reading a newspaper, oblivious to what had just occurred. Jacob stopped and listened for the sound of footsteps. *Nothing.* He let out a raggedy sigh.

Finally, a train pulled up, and Jacob got on. He didn't relax until the doors closed and the train pulled away from the platform. Even then, his hands were still shaking.

"

CHAPTER EIGHTEEN

The Biltmore Room at Grand Central was also known as the Kissing Gallery. It was a room built under the Biltmore where incoming guests could ascend directly to the hotel without going outside. A designated greeting room, it had gained its nickname many years ago. Kissing hadn't been permitted in other areas of the station for propriety and preventing traffic jams. Elka smiled to herself as she anticipated meeting Jacob there in just a few more minutes. She couldn't wait to see him, and she was definitely planning to kiss him.

Elka grabbed the suitcase stashed under her seat and exited the train. Then she followed the crowd of early morning commuters coming into the city from the suburbs. She felt buoyant as the heavy weariness that descended upon her whenever she spent time with her parents began to lift. Danbury didn't feel like home. Three days had been long enough. However, it hadn't all been bad. Her skin was a deep shade of bronze after some pleasant hours spent in a lounge chair by the pool with Colleen.

Back in her modeling days, her father worked as an investor using Elka's earnings. It seemed as though some of those investments had paid off. He was now retired and residing with her mother in a lovely home with a pool. They lived well and traveled often. So it seemed to Elka that they could afford to help with her college tuition if they really wanted to. Why they wouldn't help was something she couldn't understand.

It was as if they'd placed each of their daughters in a box. Elka was the designated pretty daughter, and her sister, the smart one. Any attempt Elka took to try and move out of her assigned box was met with resistance. For the most part, she'd simply accepted the idea that she couldn't do anything to change the way they thought about her, and Elka knew it was unlikely that even a dime of the money she'd earned modeling would ever come to her. Living in New York on her own was freeing. She could be who she wanted.

Jacob sat reading a book when Elka entered the Biltmore Room. A bouquet of red roses lay next to him on the bench. He was a sweetheart. She paused and took a moment to appreciate his appearance. A dark lock of hair hung over his eyes as he looked down at the page he was reading, unaware of her presence. There was something so beautiful about his face. It wasn't just the strong cheekbones and perfect symmetry. Jacob drew others to him through his warmth and kindness.

Elka moved closer then set down her suitcase by his feet. "What are you reading?"

Jacob's eyes met hers, and his mouth curved into a smile. He stood and wrapped his arms around her. Elka melted into his arms. She loved the way she felt when she was close to him. And when they kissed, everything was right. When she pulled away, Jacob grinned and gave her a wink.

"Ah, yes ... The Kissing Gallery." Then he held up his book to show Elka. "*To Kill a Mockingbird.*"

"Good choice."

"I think so. It's my third time reading it." He put the book down, picked up the roses, and handed them to Elka. "Oh, yeah ... I got these for you."

"They're beautiful. Thank you." She inhaled their sweet fragrance. "Are you ready for some breakfast in the park?"

After stashing her suitcase and the roses in the employee lounge at the Biltmore, they walked to Bryant Park, stopping along the way to pick up coffee and bagels. On the walk, Elka listened as Jacob relayed the events from the night before. She shivered as the thought of how close he'd been to something terrible happening to him sunk in.

"Hey, I'm okay." He paused. "They only got my wallet. I wasn't even carrying much cash. I saw some street kids when I walked out of the club. There was a girl with them who seemed kind of young, and she had a lot of freckles, so I did a double take when I saw her, wondering if she might be Olivia. One of the guys had it out for me after that."

"It could have been Olivia?" Elka tried not to get too excited. Jacob had never even seen a picture of the teen. How could he know? "What was she wearing?"

"Oh, I don't usually notice those things ... but this girl was wearing an unusual patchwork jacket that looked like an old quilt."

Adrenaline surged through Elka's body. She'd given Olivia her patchwork coat a couple of weeks after the girl had first admired it. "I'll go there after I get off work tonight."

"Please, can you wait for me? I'll go with you, but I don't get off until ten."

Elka frowned. She didn't want to wait that long. If Olivia was hanging out with kids who held people up with knives, she was definitely in trouble. "Tell you what. I'll call Mr. Sawyer and see if he'll go with me."

Mr. Sawyer steered his Chrysler Plymouth around a tipped over garbage can and pulled up to the curb. He put the car in park and took his keys from the ignition. "We're here." He pointed toward a group of grubby two-story Italianate walk-ups across the street. "It's the one with the sign that says, Hope House." The concrete steps leading up to it were crumbling, but the cheery red geraniums in the window box gave some evidence of care.

Mr. Sawyer got out of the car, and Elka followed. "You think Olivia could be here? What is this place?"

"It's an emergency shelter for homeless youth. Even if she's not, someone may know something."

A young man wearing a clerical collar opened the door before either of them had a chance to knock. He raised his eyebrows when he saw them. "Oh, hi ... can I help you with something?"

Mr. Sawyer offered a handshake. "Dale Sawyer. We're searching for a girl who goes by the name Olivia. A friend of mine sent us your way. He mentioned you help runaway teens."

"Father Bryan," he said, in a guarded tone. "I was just on my way out. Who's the friend who sent you?"

"Detective Davis. I used to work with him at the Seventeenth Precinct before I retired. This lady," he gestured toward Elka. "... is a friend of Olivia's, and she wants to talk to her ... find out if she's safe."

Elka held out her hand and smiled. "Elka Hansen." She could sense some reluctance coming from Father Bryan. It was probably a protectiveness over the kids he helped, and for that, she could hardly fault him.

"Nobody is living here who goes by that name, but then again, many of our kids go by assumed names. Can you please describe her?"

Elka gave a description and explained her interest in helping see Olivia to safety.

Father Bryan moved toward the steps leading down to the street. "I don't mean to be evasive, but many of the kids we serve have run away from home for a reason. They come from unsafe situations. Maintaining trust is important. I might be able to help you, but I'll tell you that we don't have anyone here that matches your description. I'll ask around. Why don't you leave me a way to contact you, and we'll go from there."

Elka wrote the phone number for Morgan Hall on a piece of paper and handed it to him. "Thank you."

Father Bryan took the paper and put it in his pocket. "I sincerely hope you find Olivia. It seems as though she's blessed to have you in her corner." He looked at his watch. "I really should be going now."

When he was gone, Mr. Sawyer put his hand on Elka's back in a comforting gesture. "So, should we walk around a little—talk to more people?"

"Yes. Please. And thank you so much for helping me—for driving—for your time." Elka was starting to think of Mr. Sawyer as a sort of surrogate grandparent. She'd never known her real ones. "Should we go over to that park?"

It was nearly eight in the evening, and dusk was starting to set in. After getting up early to catch the train into the city, working a full shift in the Palm Court, and then searching for Olivia, she was running out of energy. And she didn't want to exploit Mr. Sawyer's kindness. He was probably tired too. The park would need to be the last stop on their itinerary.

They crossed the street and entered through a gate into the park, a small green space with a couple of picnic tables, a slide, and a merry-go-round. It seemed strange to Elka that no children were playing outside on a summer night like this. But then she noticed the discarded needles on the ground, the broken glass, and other garbage. This was no place for children.

On the basketball court across from the playground, a few teenage boys played a game of shirts versus skin, while a couple of girls sat on the grass, watching. A patchwork coat lay next to them on the ground. The girls' backs were toward Elka.

She tried to appear casual as she approached, but when she got closer, and one of the girls turned her face to the side, Elka's excitement got the better of her. "Olivia!"

Olivia turned. Her dark kohl-rimmed eyes widened with surprise. "Elka, what are you doing here?" She got up, brushed some dead grass from her legs, and came nearer. She wore skimpy clothing and a pair of high heels that were too big, giving her the appearance of a child playing dress-up. Her wary motions indicated she was deciding whether to trust Elka. Olivia's friend stayed where she was, but she closely observed everything, and she held a defensive posture. Then Olivia's attention shifted toward Mr. Sawyer, who was standing nearby. Her eyes narrowed, and she bit her bottom lip.

Elka wanted to reassure the girl, to tell her everything was going to be okay and that she should just come home. But she knew it wasn't that simple. "Olivia, this is my friend, Mr. Sawyer. We're not here to cause trouble or anything. I've been concerned about you, and I've been looking for you. I wanted to know if you were okay."

Olivia crossed her arms. "I'm fine. You don't need to worry. I always find a couch to sleep on at night, and I'm not going back."

"Can we talk?"

"Sure. But like I said, I'm not going home."

CHAPTER NINETEEN

The Italian garden on the Biltmore's rooftop was one of Jacob's favorite places to catch a moment of peace and enjoy a reprieve from the scorching summer heat radiating off the streets below. He and Elka often chose to meet at that oasis amid concrete and steel when their breaks overlapped, as they did today.

Elka, wearing large black sunglasses, and sipping a glass of lemonade under an umbrella table near the fountain, was alone when Jacob found her. Most of the time, it was easy to forget about her former life as a model, but at this moment, she appeared as if she'd stepped straight from the cover of a glossy magazine.

Sitting down in a chair next to Elka, Jacob pulled the tab on his can of Coke and took a long drink. The cold sweet liquid revived him. "So, how did your search go last night?"

"We found Olivia." Elka sighed and leaned back in her chair. "She's okay—I think—but she refused to come home. She had a friend with her —a girl named Elise. We convinced both of them to go to a shelter called Hope House. It's not a long-term solution, but it was the best we could do for now."

"Hope House? I think there's a shelter in Seattle that goes by the same name. I wonder if they're connected." Jacob took Elka's hand in his. "Thank God you found her. That's good news."

Was Hope House the place his mother mentioned the last time they'd spoken on the phone? That would be a strange coincidence. His mother had only been retired from teaching for six months before deciding she had too much time on her hands and had sought out volunteer work helping troubled teens.

"Yes. A Hope House in Seattle? How curious. I didn't know about it until yesterday. Mr. Sawyer suggested we go there. We met a man—I think he's a Catholic priest. He seemed to be in charge. His name is Father Bryan." Elka paused and stirred her lemonade with the straw. "I haven't gone to mass in a long time. My family stopped going when we moved to New York. And now, I'm usually at work on Sundays. I've missed it." She massaged the side of her glass with her thumb. "We've never talked about religion before. Are you Catholic too?"

Jacob toyed with the medallion hanging from a chain around his neck. His mother had given it to him before he'd left home to attend Columbia. "I am. How'd you guess?"

Elka gently reached for the medallion. "Saint Thomas Aquinas, patron saint of scholars. Right?"

"Yes." He smiled. He was ashamed to admit he'd rarely been to mass since moving to New York, but lately, he'd been feeling something like a pull, drawing him back toward the faith of his childhood. "We could go to an early mass at St. Patrick's tomorrow morning ..."

Elka leaned back in her chair. "Yes, let's do that. St. Patrick's is close by. I have time to go before my shift." She bit her bottom lip as she appeared deep in thought. "I'm conflicted on what to do about Olivia. She doesn't want me to tell the authorities where she is, but even if her parents are awful people as she says, I imagine they've got to be worried sick about her. They deserve to know, right? But I'm worried that if I report her, I'll lose her trust, and she could just run away again. And the next time, she might be gone for good. At least where she is right now, she's safer than she was before. The things she told me about what she'd been doing these past few weeks ..."

Jacob nodded. He understood her dilemma, but he also felt compelled to lay it out straight.

"If you don't report her, and it's later discovered that you helped her, you could be accused of contributing to the delinquency of a minor." He didn't want Elka to get into any trouble over this. "Did Mr. Sawyer have any suggestions?"

"He said the same, essentially." Elka frowned. "I know what you're both telling me is true. But it doesn't make it any easier to do the right thing."

"I get it. I really do." Jacob paused. "What about Hope House? Won't they report her?"

"I don't think so. That's probably the only reason Olivia agreed to stay there for now." Elka spoke slowly as if she was choosing her words carefully. Her eyes focused on the little brown sparrows playing in the fountain. "Do you believe in coincidence? Or do you think God prepares everything in advance?"

"A little of both, I guess. Why do you ask?"

"I don't know. I've just been thinking about everything that's happened over the past few months ... how we ended up together ... how I met Olivia ... that sort of thing." Elka smiled. "It just seems too perfect to be a coincidence sometimes." She laughed. "Sorry. I don't mean to get all philosophical on you."

Jacob took Elka's hand and kissed it. The sparrows had caught his attention too. As they flitted about, he thought of the old hymn.

"Let not your heart be troubled," His tender word I hear,
And resting on His goodness, I lose my doubts and fears;
Though by the path He leadeth, but one step I may see;
His eye is on the sparrow, and I know He watches me..."

Elka had voiced the same question that had been rolling around in his head. He'd never before met a girl like her. "No apology needed. I like the questions you bring up, and I'm glad we're going to mass tomorrow. I need to get back to work now, but I'll see you in the morning."

After Jacob went back downstairs to the Guard Room, he kept thinking about Elka's questions. Maybe God really was a part of bringing him and Elka together. Jacob had always felt too insignificant to bother God with the little details of his life. He figured God had more important problems to be concerned with. But if it were true that God was working behind the scenes in people's lives, then maybe God wouldn't mind if he prayed and asked for some guidance on how to keep Elka in his life. Seattle? New York? Viet Nam? No matter what his future held, Jacob wanted Elka to be a part of it.

Jacob took off his hat as he and Elka entered through St. Patrick's Cathedral's enormous bronze doors on Sunday morning. The sound of a choir, accompanied by bells, greeted them. The white marble arches drew his eye toward the incredible stained glass windows. Jacob felt like he'd entered another world, leaving the gritty streets behind. He followed Elka in making the sign of the cross as they moved farther into the sanctuary.

Though it had been a long time since he'd attended mass, Jacob felt his body relax, as if he'd come home. Elka chose a spot for them to sit near the back. A few sideways glances gave Jacob the impression that Elka's feelings about being here matched his own. It was a comfort to realize that they had this connection in common. He wanted to talk more about it with her, but neither spoke to each other for the next hour. Instead, they participated in the ancient liturgy, along with hundreds of other churchgoers, a part of something bigger than themselves.

After the service, Jacob walked back toward the Biltmore with Elka. She needed to be at work in less than thirty minutes. He wished they had more time to spend together. Elka was unusually quiet. "What's on your mind?"

Elka smiled and reached for Jacob's hand. "I was thinking about Hope House ... Olivia, and the other kids who are there. I want to help somehow."

"Oh? What were you thinking?" Jacob frowned. His thoughts went straight to the memory of being followed and then robbed in that neighborhood. It was one thing for Elka to go there with Mr. Sawyer, quite another to go alone.

"I don't know. I got out of modeling because I wanted to do something more important with my life. But what am I doing now? Being a hostess in the Palm Court isn't quite what I had in mind. I feel like I'm treading water and not going anywhere." She paused. "To keep things running around the clock, some of the staff live at Hope House. I wonder if they would take me?"

"It's not safe. Don't you remember what happened to me the other night?"

Elka drew her eyebrows up. "Safe? I remember. And I'm sorry that happened to you. But I'm not going to let that stop me." She dropped Jacob's hand. A coolness settled in between them as they walked the next block in silence.

Jacob chose his next words carefully. "I'm sorry. I don't mean to be critical. It's just ... I care about you."

"My father said the same thing to me when I wanted to quit modeling and go to college. But what he really cared about was losing his meal ticket."

Ouch. Elka was comparing him to her father now? That was a low blow. Jacob was relieved when they'd reached the Biltmore, and it was time to part ways. Elka carried deep scars from her past, and he was trying his best to understand where she was coming from, but she'd completely distorted his concern for something else.

Jacob didn't respond to Elka's comment. They rode the elevator together in silence. When the doors opened, she turned toward the employee locker room, mumbling a quick good-bye as she left.

CHAPTER TWENTY

The door to Hope House was ajar when Elka arrived on Monday morning. She could hear voices talking, laughter, a vacuum cleaner running, and the clomping of feet on stairs. Feeling awkward and wondering what to do next, Elka raised her hand toward the door. This time she was alone, but just as before, the door swung inward before she had a chance to knock. But instead of the priest, a young woman was on her way out. Both women jumped in surprise as they nearly collided.

"Oh, hello," the woman said as she continued past Elka and down the stairs. "Go on in. If you need Father Bryan, he's in the kitchen."

Elka stepped inside the front hallway and surveyed the space. How many people lived here? Though a bit dingy, the place had the feel of a busy yet comfortable family home. The kitchen was likely toward the back of the house. Elka moved in that direction. The smell of coffee and bacon wafted toward her, an indication she was going the right way. Two teenage boys passed her in the hallway. Both greeted her but didn't seem particularly curious about her presence. It was as if strangers were a regular presence here.

It had been three nights since Elka and Mr. Sawyer had found Olivia and her friend Elise at the park, then brought them to Hope House. That evening, her focus had been on the girls and getting them to safety. But now, she took in every detail of this home, which served as a refuge for street kids. It was impressive. Where did the money come from to run this place?

Elka already knew what she needed to do, but she wanted to talk with Olivia first. She found the kitchen, and sure enough, there stood Father Bryan, his hands submerged in a sink full of suds and dishes. Next to him, drying dishes, was Olivia. "Father Bryan, Olivia ... do you need any help?" Elka asked. The pile of still unwashed dirty dishes was considerable.

"Good morning, Elka. Actually, I'll let you take over for me. I have a meeting at the parks department in a half hour that I need to get to. Thank you." Father Bryan wiped his hands dry on a towel.

Olivia glanced at Elka and gave a shy smile. "They put you to work right away when you come here."

"I see that." Elka grabbed a sticky plate, covered in syrup, and plunged it into the hot soapy water. "How are you doing?"

"There are a lot of rules here, but it's not so bad." Olivia opened a cupboard and put away a stack of bowls. "Elise left. She said she'd rather be free to do what she wants. I thought you would come back. It's why I stayed."

Elka cleared her throat, which suddenly felt thick with emotion. They finished up the dishes over the next few minutes, making small talk as they worked. With a revolving cast of characters coming in and out of the kitchen the entire time, it didn't seem the right time or place to have a serious conversation. Hope House was a friendly place, but there wasn't a lot of privacy.

A screen door on the back wall led to a small yellow patch of grass outside the kitchen. A couple of tomato plants were growing in pots on the steps. Bed sheets fluttered in the breeze as they dried on a clothesline. A tall brick wall and the neighboring buildings gave the area some shade.

Elka pointed toward the door. "Do you want to sit and talk out there?" Olivia nodded in reply.

It was only mid-morning, but already, it was getting hot. They sat together on the porch steps. Olivia picked off some dead leaves from one of the tomato plants. "I guess you want to know why I ran away."

"Yes. What happened?"

"My mom has a new boyfriend. His name is Harold. He wanted us to move to his house in New Jersey. He's a real creep, and there's no way I'm going to live with him." Olivia was quiet. The silence between words and the things left unsaid told Elka everything else she needed to know. Her stomach hurt, and she pushed away a painful memory of a photographer, a dark room, and a couch.

Olivia's voice shook as she continued. "I told my mom how I felt about him, but she wouldn't listen. The night before I was supposed to leave for summer camp, we got in a big fight. She was drunk. In the morning, she was still passed out when it was time to leave. I thought she was going to drive me, but I couldn't even wake her up. The camp bus was leaving my school, and even though I ran and tried to get there on time, I was too late. It left without me. I really wanted to go to camp." Olivia hugged her knees to her chest. "That was when I decided I wasn't going home."

Elka put her arm around Olivia's shoulder. "I'm so sorry, sweetie." She could feel Olivia's tense muscles relax after about a minute of quiet—except for a siren in the distance and a couple of birds singing.

"What happened to you ... it's not okay." Elka said, breaking the silence. "You have people who are worried about you, who care, people who will help—if they know the truth." Elka took a deep breath. "I need to be straight with you. I have to tell Mrs. Nadington where you are. You can't stay here forever, and it's not safe for you to be living on the streets. Will you please let me help you?"

Olivia didn't answer right away. She seemed to be thinking. "Okay. But if I have to live with Harold, I'm gone."

Elka nodded and said a silent prayer. *Please, God, show me what to do.*

Belvedere Castle in Central Park held a sense of romanticism and wonderment for Elka. She remembered the first time she'd been here, shortly after moving to New York. Colleen had been with her. The sisters had been exploring The Ramble when they discovered the place. It was more of an open-air vista than an actual castle, but it looked dreamy from a distance.

Later that day, Elka had thrown a coin in the Bethesda fountain. Sixteen at the time, her wish had been specific—to someday return to this magical spot with her prince. Maybe not a literal prince but definitely someone who treated her like a princess. A man who was kind and generous, who loved her unconditionally, and made her laugh. And if he was attractive, with dark hair, blue eyes, and a smile that made her heart beat faster, all the better.

Elka followed Jacob along the pathway toward the tower. Was Jacob her wish come true? She no longer believed in fairy tales. But Jacob, he was everything she wanted. Except he was leaving in a few weeks. Would their relationship last after that?

Jacob had graciously accepted Elka's apology for the rude way she'd spoken to him on Sunday morning after mass. She was ashamed for misreading his concern for her safety. Her reaction had been over-the-top and ridiculous. Gratitude filled her heart that he'd been so understanding. Yesterday morning, before she left to visit Olivia at Hope House, they had breakfast together, and he'd given her a small can of mace.

"Every city girl should have one of these," he said. "I'll feel better if you have it with you."

They were at Belvedere Castle now. Sadly, vandals had covered much of it with graffiti. She tried not to be disappointed. Elka ignored the grubbiness right in front of her and took in the sweeping views of the park instead. "Belvedere means beautiful view."

Jacob took Elka's hand in his own. "That it is. I'm going to miss living here."

Elka didn't want to think about Jacob leaving. "Do you want to walk over to the fountain?"

"Sure. Do you want to tell me how it went yesterday with Olivia?"

"I took her to Mrs. Nadington at the Children's Aid Society." Elka stepped gingerly as she made her way down the steeply sloped dirt pathway. Her ankle was better now, and she intended to keep it that way. "She went willingly, but it was a hard day. It's not a good situation in her home. She's in temporary foster care right now. I wanted to take her to my place, but there are all sorts of rules about that kind of thing. I'd have to be licensed. Not to mention, "home" is a single room at Morgan Hall."

"I'm glad you could help her." Jacob paused. "There's been something I've wanted to ask you. Have you ever considered living in Seattle?"

Seattle? Elka felt her breath hitch. This was an abrupt change in topic. "Oh ... well, I don't know. It's so far. My sister, and now Olivia ..." He'd caught her off-guard.

Jacob stopped walking and gestured toward a bench. "Do you want to sit down?" Elka nodded. "I'm sorry. That was kind of sudden. I didn't mean to spring such a big question on you like that. It's—it's just something to think about."

Elka tried to gather her composure. She could tell her response hadn't been what Jacob had been hoping for. The realization hit that she really did love him. Of course, moving to Seattle would make sense if they were going to have a future together. And that's what she wanted. Right?

But this felt wrong. She studied a dirty spot on the toe of her white Keds. Something was missing. He'd never said, *I love you*. She wasn't going to Seattle until Jacob uttered those three little words. Until now, she hadn't realized how much she'd been longing to hear him say it. Elka leaned over and kissed him lightly on the cheek. "I'll think about it."

CHAPTER TWENTY-ONE

Jacob gathered his nickels, dimes, and quarters from the top of his dresser and dropped them in his pocket. It was only enough for a short call. He took the elevator down to the lobby where the payphones offered more privacy than the one in the employee lounge.

The lobby was quiet for a mid-morning in July. But then again, business travel was lighter during the summer, and the tourists were more prevalent on the weekends. Was it too early to make a call? Jacob glanced at his watch—ten-fifteen, which meant it was seven-fifteen in Seattle. It wasn't too early for his mom, who had likely been up for several hours already.

Jacob picked up the black receiver and dialed zero. A woman's voice came on the line. "Operator speaking. How may I place your call?" After plunking the appropriate number of coins in the slots, Jacob waited for someone to answer. Being the last of his siblings to leave home, it would likely be either his mother or Betty, their housekeeper. His father was probably already on the golf course.

"Hello, this is Ann Lewis speaking."

"Hi, Mom." Jacob leaned against the wall. "I'm coming home in a month. Are you ready for me?"

"Of course, dear. Your father and I are looking forward to it—your sisters too. Send me your flight information so we know when to pick you up." Claire and MaryAnne were both married, had two kids each, and lived in Seattle. It had been a year since he'd seen them. "How's your summer going?" his mother asked.

"Good. I've been working a lot, trying to save up some money for school."

"Are you still seeing that lovely girl we met? The model—Elka? How's she doing? Is she still on crutches?"

Jacob twisted the phone cord around his finger and smiled. "Our work schedules make it difficult to see each other as much as I'd like, but yesterday we went on a long walk through Central Park. It was nice, and no, she doesn't have the crutches anymore."

"Ah, ha ... good." Jacob knew from her tone that his mother was smiling. "You know, your father was talking to a friend at Broadmoor about you. Apparently, there's an opening in the dining room for an experienced waiter. You should apply."

"Thank you. I'll do that."

"And your friend, Elka. Why don't you invite her to come to Seattle for a week? Maybe she'll want to stay. Bring her before school starts and you get too busy. What do you think?"

Jacob took a deep breath. His mother always meant well, even if she could be a tad intrusive when it came to his love life. Yes, it would have made more sense for him to first extend an invitation to Elka to visit Seattle before asking her if she'd consider living there. What was he thinking? Asking Elka if she'd consider moving across the country to a city she'd never been to was nuts. They'd only been dating for three months, and her life was in New York. He'd clearly spooked her yesterday, and he was now feeling like a fool. "I don't know, Mom. I'll think about it."

"Sure, honey. Let me know."

"Please insert another ten cents to continue your call," the operator said, cutting them off.

Jacob had used up his change. "Sorry, Mom. I'm out of money. Have to go. Love you." The line went dead. Jacob put the receiver back on the hook.

Taking the stairs instead of the elevator, Jacob mulled over his mom's suggestion as he made his way back to his room. He and Elka could go out to dinner, someplace nice and romantic. The Rainbow Room? And then, he could ask her to come to Seattle for a week.

Should he buy a plane ticket first and then offer it to her as a gift? What if she said no? Could he even afford the airfare? It was going to be a stretch, but she was worth it. With each day that passed, Jacob was growing more confident that Elka was the girl for him. Forever. He loved her. Jacob was sure of it. She was everything he'd ever wanted in a lifelong partner. Being with her made him happy. But did Elka feel the same way about him?

By the time Jacob reached the twenty-sixth floor, he was huffing and out of breath. But he had a plan—a candlelight dinner and a gift-wrapped box with a ticket. Seattle was beautiful in August. Elka would love it, he hoped. Jacob smiled to himself. This time, he'd thought of everything.

Morgan Hall's lobby was as far as Jacob was ever allowed to go when he visited Elka. Morgan Hall was a YWCA building, and there were strict rules for the women who lived here. He waved to Ms. Grover, the stern woman at the front desk who made sure those rules were followed. Jacob found a chair by the front window and made himself comfortable while waiting for Elka to come downstairs.

It had been almost a week since he'd devised his plan to surprise Elka with a trip to Seattle. Keeping it a secret hadn't been easy. She only knew they were going out to dinner tonight. Jacob had been forced to come up with a quick excuse for why he couldn't go to the library with her this afternoon when she'd asked. Ordinarily, they spent Tuesday afternoons together, but today he had an important errand to run. It was an appointment at the travel agency to pick up the tickets, but Jacob couldn't tell Elka that. Instead, he'd mumbled an explanation about needing to do his laundry. He wasn't sure if she'd bought it or not.

Elka agreed to meet him in the lobby at six. Right now, according to the clock on the wall, it was five till. Jacob checked the inside of his suit jacket again. The tickets were still there. Maybe he should have given Elka a hint that tonight's restaurant would be more formal than the usual pizza joints they frequented on date nights. She always dressed up for dates, though, and looked like a million bucks, so his failure to mention a dress code was unlikely to be a problem.

"Hey, Jacob," a familiar voice said, startling him from his thoughts. "How's it going?" Colleen dropped her bag on the floor and took a chair nearby.

"Oh, hey, Colleen. When did you get here?" He pasted a smile on his face. Ordinarily, he would have been happy to see Colleen. But not now. His gut told him, this evening's well-laid plans were about to be altered.

"Just arrived. I thought I'd surprise my sister. Is she on her way downstairs? Or should I go up and get her?" Colleen didn't wait for an answer. Instead, she waved a hand toward Jacob. "You're all dressed up. You two didn't have special plans or anything tonight, did you?"

Jacob was about to answer when he saw Elka coming down the staircase. His eyes lingered for a moment as he took in the simple but elegant white sundress she was wearing. It showed off her long, deeply tanned legs.

Elka seemed as surprised as Jacob had been to find Colleen sitting there. "Colleen?"

Colleen rushed toward her sister. Elka wrapped her arms protectively around the younger girl. She quirked an eyebrow as she made eye contact with Jacob. He hitched his shoulder and shook his head. He didn't know any more about the surprise visit than she did.

After a good ten seconds, Colleen finally broke her hold on Elka. "I'm sorry. I wanted to surprise you. I wasn't thinking. You were on your way out. Go on. Don't worry about me. I'll wait here."

Elka looked between Colleen and Jacob, her eyes expressing conflict and confusion. Jacob sensed what he needed to say next. "It's okay. We can reschedule. I understand." Regret washed over him as soon as the compromise slipped through his lips.

Elka mouthed the words, *thank you*, to Jacob. What else could he do? He tried his best to keep his face neutral and hide his disappointment.

Colleen gave an apologetic glance toward Jacob, but she seemed visibly relieved. "Are you sure? We could all get something to eat together. Anyone up for pizza?"

Not really. But Jacob didn't say that. Instead, he gave a quick nod. "I'll be right back. I need to make a quick phone call." He'd cancel their reservation at the Rainbow Room.

After dinner, Jacob walked back to the Biltmore along Forty-Fifth, wondering if he would even have another opportunity to be alone with Elka before he'd finished his stay in New York. As soon as the pizza arrived at their table, Colleen had announced her intention to apply for a job at the Biltmore. She wanted to stay in the city for the rest of the summer with her sister.

It had been a disappointing evening, and Elka's ticket to Seattle was still in Jacob's pocket.

CHAPTER TWENTY-TWO

Elka knocked on the door to Mrs. Nadington's office and waited for an answer. Even though she'd already proven herself responsible in her volunteer work here, Elka's stomach felt unsettled, and her hands were shaky. The outcome of this meeting could change her life, and she wanted to make a good impression.

"Come in," a voice on the other side of the door called out. Elka entered the small window-less room and greeted the Children's Aid Society director. "Have a seat, Elka. What can I do for you?" she asked in a businesslike tone.

Elka sat on the edge of the chair and held tightly to her purse. "I would like to be licensed as a foster parent. What do I need to do?"

Mrs. Nadington removed her glasses and set them on the desk. She sat back in her chair and steepled her hands. Elka felt like she was being scrutinized. "Olivia has adjusted remarkably well over the last few days, and her current foster parents have expressed a desire to keep her in their home for as long as necessary. I'm sure that if you'd like to see her, I could arrange something." Mrs. Nadington narrowed her eyes. "Tell me, are you interested in providing foster care in general, or specifically for Olivia?"

"Well, I was thinking for Olivia." Elka paused. "She's happy?"

Leaning forward, Mrs. Nadington held eye contact with an intense gaze that made Elka squirm. "That girl has been through a lot, but I believe she can be, eventually."

Elka nodded, remembering the last time she'd seen Olivia. Shortly after bringing the runaway teen to Mrs. Nadington, she'd been forced to say goodbye. The ache in her heart has been almost unbearable. The courage Olivia had shown in telling her story, the vulnerability, and the fear of the unknown, so bravely met, had clarified Elka's resolve like nothing else.

That feeling of aimlessness, resting like a cloud over her for the last few years, vanished at that moment. Elka knew her life's purpose had something to do with helping girls like Olivia—something beyond after-school tutoring. "I know I don't have a lot to offer right now. I live in a single room at Morgan Hall. But I can find my own place."

"You're very young, and you're not married. Honey, I'll be honest. Being a foster parent is probably not the right move for you right now, even though I admire your heart and your intentions. Wait a few years. There will always be more kids like Olivia who need an ally like you on their side."

Hot tears prickled at the corners of Elka's eyes, threatening to spill. She swallowed hard and took a deep breath. Mrs. Nadington's face showed compassion, and though Elka didn't like what the woman said, there was some truth to her words. The guilt would have been unbearable if she hadn't at least made an effort to provide a home for Olivia. But if it was true, and Olivia was in a good home right now, maybe Elka had done all she could for the girl.

"She's really okay?" Elka searched Mrs. Nadington's eyes for confirmation.

"Yes. You would have enjoyed seeing the smile on Olivia's face when she met the puppy who also lives in her new home. It's a little bulldog—the cutest thing ever—named Max. The two of them seem to share a special connection." Mrs. Nadington smiled. "I hope you'll continue volunteering with our after-school tutoring program this fall."

Elka nodded noncommittally. "Thank you. I'm not sure what my schedule will be like in the fall. I'm back to working in the Palm Court, which has different hours. I'll let you know."

The phone on the director's desk rang. "I better take this." She put her hand on the receiver. "I'm glad you came by."

Elka stood and offered a handshake to Mrs. Nadington before leaving. She felt a strange mixture of sorrow and relief.

Colleen was the only person who knew about her plans to come here today. When Elka had told her sister what she was thinking about doing for Olivia, Colleen was excited. Her exact words were, *We could all live together! It'll be like a sorority.* Elka had nearly rolled her eyes in response to that, but she'd said nothing. Olivia needed someone to mother her more than she needed a sorority sister. And Colleen? If she wanted to join a sorority, there were plenty of options for that at Barnard.

The rules at Morgan Hall, which prohibited overnight guests, had been stretched a few times over the past year when Elka allowed her sister to stay in her room, but she wasn't going to push her luck too much with management. The risk of getting both of them thrown out was real. Before she left this morning, Elka had informed Colleen that if she planned on staying another night, she'd have to rent her own room. Having her sister around was great and all, but Elka was already longing for some privacy.

Elka exited the building and stood for a moment, deciding whether to walk over to the Biltmore and see Jacob or return home. It was still early, and she didn't need to work for a couple of hours yet.

It hadn't been Elka's intention to keep the idea of providing a foster home for Olivia a secret from Jacob. She was going to talk to him about it at dinner last night, but then Colleen had shown up, and it hadn't seemed the right time or place to bring it up. And now it was a moot topic.

There was still the whole unanswered question about going to Seattle that she'd promised Jacob she'd think about. The outcome of today's meeting with Mrs. Nadington may have cleared one of the roadblocks in Elka's way, but it hadn't been the only one. There were more.

The next day, Elka met Jacob for breakfast at the automat. He was waiting for her at a table near the back when she arrived. Jacob stood and greeted her with a smile. Elka waved and made her way over to where he was.

She gave him a quick kiss on the cheek. "Were you waiting long?"

"No, I just got here. There aren't many tables left. Do you want to wait here? I can get breakfast."

"Sure." Elka slid onto her chair and settled in.

"The usual?"

"Yes, thank you."

Jacob was back in five minutes. He set down a tray with two black coffees, a bowl of plain yogurt, a hard-boiled egg, and toast for Elka, and a bagel with cream cheese for himself.

"Thank you. This looks good." Elka brought the coffee mug close and inhaled the delicious aroma before taking a sip.

Jacob glanced toward the entrance. "Will your sister be joining us this morning?"

"She went home yesterday. There weren't any extra rooms available at Morgan Hall and not many jobs available that she was qualified for at the Biltmore. She'll be fine. Anyway, she only has a few weeks left until she moves into her dorm at Barnard."

Jacob's eyebrows shot up for a moment, then he quickly looked away.

Elka laughed. "It's okay. I get it. Frankly, I'm a bit relieved too. I love my sister, but we're running out of time before you need to go back to Seattle. I don't want to share the time I have left with you." She took a bite of yogurt. "And I wanted to apologize for the other night when Colleen's arrival spoiled our plans. Thank you for including her."

"No problem." Jacob shifted in his chair, his blue eyes focusing on her. His frown contradicted his verbal response, and Elka sensed he was holding something back. Jacob poured some sugar into his coffee. "So what's new?"

Elka put down her coffee mug. "I spoke with Mrs. Nadington yesterday at the Children's Aid Society. I wanted to see how Olivia was doing, and I also wanted to discuss getting a license to be a foster parent.

Jacob's mouth dropped open. He was quiet for a moment. "That's a ... a big step to take. And how is Olivia?"

"Apparently, she's got a new puppy at the home she's at. Mrs. Nadington says Olivia is doing well. And no, I'm not going to be a foster parent—at least, not right now."

"Ah, ha. Well ..." Jacob still seemed to be trying to regain his composure.

"But I'm still thinking about volunteering at Hope House."

"I see." Jacob was unreadable. His expression was neutral.

Elka wanted to see some kind of emotion, a clue to what he was feeling. If he really wanted her to go to Seattle with him, why was he so passive? "Please, tell me what you're thinking."

"What I'm thinking?" Jacob bit his bottom lip. "Sometimes, I wonder if you're using your sister and Olivia to keep me at a distance."

"What?" Elka pushed her plate away. "No, I don't think ..." She didn't finish her sentence. Jacob was standing up from the table now, preparing to leave.

"I love you, Elka." Jacob gathered his things. He seemed more hurt than angry. "I'll talk to you later." And then he left.

There, he'd said the words Elka had been waiting to hear. But this wasn't at all the way she'd wanted to receive them. Not wanting to break down in public, Elka fought back burning tears.

Was he right?

Had she been using the drama in Colleen's and Olivia's lives to avoid getting too close to Jacob?

CHAPTER TWENTY-THREE

Taking a book with him, Jacob went to the rooftop garden. He didn't really want to read. He needed some time to think. But having a book along would help him blend in and hopefully discourage anyone who wanted to talk from approaching him. It was an old cowboy novel he'd found in the employee lounge. He didn't even like cowboy novels.

After five minutes of staring at the same page, Jacob glanced up and watched what was happening around him instead. A pair of white doves were splashing in the fountain. A little girl with pigtails, probably around eight years old, was skipping around the garden's perimeter. A man, who was presumably her father, sat at a nearby picnic table under an umbrella and read a newspaper while keeping an eye on the girl.

Jacob thought about the confession he'd made to Elka at the automat. He still couldn't believe those words had come out of his mouth. Should he regret saying them out loud? He did love Elka. That much was true. He wasn't sure if he'd been fair in his assessment of the situation. What else could he expect from her?

Maybe she was right to keep him at a distance. It wasn't as if he'd made any kind of commitment to Elka. Their relationship was still so new. They hadn't yet talked about the future. If she wanted to become a foster parent or wanted to work at Hope House, what business did he have to keep her from those things?

The light scent of strawberries and citrus—Elka's perfume—brought Jacob out of his thoughts and into the present. She settled into the lounge chair beside him, reached out, and put her hand on his knee.

"There you are. Hey... can we please finish that conversation we started at breakfast?" She gave an apologetic smile. "I've been thinking about what you said. I know I'm not the easiest person to get to know. I put up barriers. I don't want it to be that way with you." Elka took off her sunglasses. Her eyes were tear-filled. "I love you too. Will you please forgive me?"

Jacob put the book down and moved closer to Elka. The tension was palpable. Of course, he'd forgive her. He wanted nothing more than to take her into his arms, right now, and kiss her. But Jacob was mindful that they were both employees in a Biltmore public space, so he refrained.

"There's nothing to forgive. I know there's a lot we need to talk about. But I want you to know, the way you care for the people in your life—the way you give of yourself to others— that's a beautiful quality. I don't want to discourage you from that, or to make you think that I don't support you."

Elka smiled and leaned against Jacob's shoulder. "I appreciate that."

"Foster-parenting, huh? How many kids do you think you want to have someday?"

"Only a dozen or so." Elka's tone was teasing, and she winked. "And you? How many kids do you want?"

"I want kids. I love being an uncle." Jacob was anxious to see his nieces and nephew again in a few weeks. A year was a long time for a kid. Would they even remember him?

Elka picked up the novel Jacob had set aside and hiked an eyebrow. "Is this any good?"

Jacob laughed. "I have no idea. I never got past the first page. Let's try a do-over. I'll call the restaurant and get a new reservation. Does next Tuesday work for you?"

"Yes, it does, and I'd like that." She stood and kissed his cheek. "Don't worry. I won't invite anyone else along this time."

Mr. Simmons greeted a party of six who'd just entered the Guard Room. Finally, some customers. From his station near the kitchen, Jacob watched, and he adjusted his tie. Surely, Mr. Simmons would seat this group in his section. Clyde and Oscar, the other waiters working tonight, each had several tables full of people.

It had been a slow evening—at least for Jacob—the kind where it hardly seemed worthwhile to have come to work at all. If there weren't any tips to be made, Jacob would prefer to spend this time with Elka. The moments they spent together were never enough, and the weeks until his big move across the country were winding down far too quickly.

Jacob had already been at work for two hours, and so far, he'd only had one table of four to serve. For some unknown reason, the maître d' had been ignoring Jacob's section all night. Mr. Simmons was a terrible snob, and he was known to be petty if he didn't like someone on staff. Jacob had always gone out of his way to avoid getting on the man's wrong side. Questioning the maître d' or asking for more customers would probably not go over so very well.

Mr. Simmons led the party of six to a table in Oscar's section. *Really?* Jacob let out a deep sigh.

Only a few more weeks, and he'd be done with this job. When the maître d' returned to his podium, Jacob wandered over for a conversation. He put on a smile and did his best to sound friendly, even though his blood was boiling. "Hey, Mr. Simmons. I've only had one table tonight. Did that last group request Oscar?"

Mr. Simmons shook his head. "I have a group of five coming in. Hopefully, any moment now. They're late." The man scowled at Jacob as if he was personally responsible for the customer's delay. "They requested you."

Jacob raised an eyebrow. "Oh? What's the name on the reservation?"

"Montclair." The maître d' sniffed.

"Robert Montclair?" Susan's parents. Would Chase be with them? It was possible. He could be home on leave right now. Had it been eight weeks already since his friend left for basic training?

The maître d' checked his book. "Yes, Robert Montclair."

"Ah. Well, thank you." Jacob wandered back to his station near the kitchen to wait for his next customers. He was looking forward to seeing the Montclair family, whether Chase was with them or not. But an opportunity to visit with his friend before he left for Nam would turn around what had been, so far, a wasted evening.

Five minutes later, Mr. and Mrs. Montclair, Chase, Susan, and her sister Andrea, entered the Guard Room. Mr. Simmons led the group to table nine. Chase was in uniform. After they were seated, Jacob walked over to greet them.

Mr. Montclair waved and called out to Jacob before he reached the table. "Jacob, old boy, I'm glad we caught you on a night you were working. How are you?"

"Very well, sir. Mrs. Montclair. Susan. Andrea. Private Freeman." Jacob grinned and gave a slap on the back to his friend. "Good to see you, man."

Chase offered a handshake. "Hey, Jacob. Good to see you too. There's nowhere else I'd rather enjoy my last steak before I ship out."

"I'll make sure that tonight will be a meal to remember." Jacob always took good care of his customers, but he was determined to go above and beyond to make this dining experience extra special for Chase and his family.

When Jacob told the chef that one of their customers was a departing soldier, the chef insisted on sending out some of his best off-the-menu specialties. Richard, the sommelier, also joined the fun, bringing out a rare vintage of Ridge Monte Bello Cabernet—all on the house.

By the time table nine was enjoying their dessert course, it was past closing. When they got up to leave, Mr. Montclair left behind a tip that more than made up for the otherwise slow evening in the dining room. Jacob had treated them well, but his motivation hadn't been the tip. He'd just wanted to honor his friend.

"Are you getting off work soon?" Chase asked Jacob as he got up to leave. "Susan and her family can go back without me. Want to catch up and get a drink in the hotel bar?"

"Yeah, that'd be great. I can be out of here in ten minutes. I'll meet you there." Jacob said goodbye to the rest of the group, then went to close out for the evening.

Jacob scanned the smoke-filled bar a while later, searching for Chase. His friend was alone in a booth near the piano. The pianist was playing "Come Fly with Me." Nearby, three middle-aged execs, who'd already had a few too many, loudly sang along off-key.

Sliding into the booth, Jacob rolled his eyes and nodded toward the singers. "Ordinarily, the talent here is better than that. So, how long are you in town for?"

Chase glanced toward the group of men and chuckled. "Two days."

The pianist finished his song and left. That was when the rowdy men took notice of Chase and Jacob. The tallest one seemed to zero in on Chase's uniform. He sneered and shook his head. Chase held up two fingers in the peace sign, but the tall man responded by giving Chase the middle finger. "You should be ashamed," the man slurred.

From there, everything escalated quickly. Jacob jumped to his friend's defense, and not long after that, Jacob felt his fist smashing into the man's face.

The bartender broke up the fight and sent everyone home. Jacob said goodbye to Chase, feeling terrible about how his friend's last hurrah in New York had ended.

Jacob wasn't sure if the bartender would report the incident or not. Fighting with guests in the hotel bar could result in his termination. If he lost his job, he'd lose his housing—and he'd have to leave for Seattle right away, losing valuable time with Elka.

CHAPTER TWENTY-FOUR

Elka took Jacob's hand as he offered to lead her to the rotating dance floor under the grand chandelier. Peter Duchin was on the piano, the twinkling cityscape views were stunning, and a romantic mood filled the room. Nothing else mattered except enjoying this moment with her man.

She leaned her head against Jacob's chest as they moved to the slow music. Elka closed her eyes and allowed Jacob to lead. He'd brought her to the Rainbow Room. This must have been where he'd planned to take her last week. She'd brushed him off in favor of pizza with her sister. Oh, how inconsiderate she'd been. The Rainbow Room was legendary for its glamor and A-list clientele. It certainly wasn't the kind of place broke college students or off-duty waiters frequented—not unless it was a really special evening. What was Jacob up to?

When the song was over, Elka and Jacob returned to their table, ready to order dessert. Elka perused the menu. "Bananas Foster, do you want to share?"

Jacob nodded. "Yes, that sounds perfect."

Elka stroked the bruised skin on Jacob's hand. Why hadn't he volunteered an explanation yet? "So, what happened?"

Jacob turned away as if embarrassed. "It's not a big deal. My friend, Chase, came into the restaurant last night with Susan and her family. He's home for a couple of days on leave. After work, we met for drinks. Some guys were disrespecting Chase because of his uniform. I don't know what came over me, but I punched one of them. I've never hit anybody before in my life." Jacob shook his head. "I was so mad. You know I'm against the war. But Chase didn't choose to enlist. It made me so mad to see him treated that way."

Elka pulled Jacob's hand to her lips and kissed it. "Does it hurt?"

"Not really. It happened at the Biltmore bar. The guy I hit had a bloody nose, but he'll be fine. I was worried I might lose my job. Joe was working in the bar and saw the whole thing as it went down. I talked to him today, and he assured me he wasn't going to say anything. His brother is over in Nam right now."

A waiter came by and took their order. When the man left, Jacob reached into the inside of his suit jacket and took his gift. He slid it across the table toward Elka with a shy smile.

"For me? What is it?"

Jacob laughed. "Open it."

Elka did as he asked. Inside the envelope, she found a round trip airline ticket to Seattle. She gasped.

Jacob's next words tumbled out. "I wasn't sure if I should surprise you or if it was presumptuous to buy a ticket without asking you if you wanted to go first. Do you want to come to Seattle? I don't want to pressure you, but I figured, if you were to consider moving to a new city, you would want to see it first. Besides, my family would love to get to know you." He'd barely taken a breath the whole time he was speaking.

Elka could sense he was nervous, and she decided to put an end to his misery. She smiled. "Thank you, and yes, I would love to visit your hometown."

She glanced at the dates on the ticket—the second week of August. That was only two weeks away. She hoped it wouldn't be a problem to get those days off work. "I'm excited to get to know your family too." Was she? She knew that was the right thing to say, but the truth was, the idea also made her feel a little anxious. What if they didn't like her?

As if he'd read her thoughts, Jacob said, "They're going to love you."

The waiter rolled a cart over to their table and began to prepare the Bananas Foster in front of them. Even though she knew what was coming, Elka still nearly jumped out of her chair when the waiter put a flame to the sauce. Her cheeks grew warm with embarrassment over the little yelp she gave at the same time, but then she laughed when she saw Jacob had reacted the same way.

Then the waiter left, allowing them to enjoy their dessert. The warm gooey goodness of the bananas and ice cream smothered in a buttery sweet sauce was just about the best thing Elka had ever tasted. "This evening has been perfect, Jacob. I mean it. Thank you."

They were on the sixty-fifth floor of Rockefeller Center. Outside the window, the view was like no other. The magical Manhattan skyline was intoxicating. She couldn't imagine living anywhere else, but she'd be willing to try for the man sitting across the table.

Her love for Jacob was real. What they'd shared over the last few months was more than a summer fling, but where was this relationship headed? Marriage? It seemed so soon to think about such things. If she moved across the country to follow him, would she be giving up too much of herself? What if she didn't like Seattle? And what about her sister? Colleen needed her here. Right? There were still so many unanswered questions.

Colleen sat on Elka's bed, brushing her hair. "I wish you didn't have to work all the time. I don't get to see you enough."

"I know. I'm sorry. I wish I could see you more often too." Elka sighed. Her sister had come to visit for the weekend. Thankfully, this time Colleen had called beforehand. Elka had already rearranged her schedule as much as possible. Skipping out of work to spend the day shopping wasn't an option. "If I could afford to, I'd ask someone else to fill in for me, and I'd spend the whole day with you, but there's something I haven't told you yet." Elka turned toward her sister and smiled. "I'm already taking all of next week off from work because I'm going to Seattle with Jacob."

Colleen's mouth fell open. "You are? That sounds like fun! So you and Jacob are getting pretty serious, huh? You're going to meet his parents?"

Elka twisted her hair into a bun. "I'm just going for a visit, and I already met his parents. Sort of. It doesn't mean I'm moving there."

"Of course not! You're a true New Yorker. You'd never consider moving." Colleen smacked a pillow for emphasis. "Would you?"

"Look, I need to get to the Biltmore. I'll be off at four. Then we can talk. Did you decide what you wanted to do tonight?"

"Why don't we go to West Village? We could find a new place to eat."

"Sounds good to me." Elka felt a pang of guilt for leaving her sister hanging, but this wasn't a good time for a long talk.

After work, Colleen wanted Elka to go to a poetry cafe called The Salty Cat. They boarded the subway for Greenwich Village and arrived at half-past seven. The coffeehouse was a dank, dark basement with a small stage, yet it was far from dull. The audience—mostly artistic, hippie types—made the place colorful. Elka was more interested in people-watching than in the performance onstage—a folk singer who rarely hit her notes.

There was no food to be had in the cafe, only some terrible, overpriced coffee, so after less than an hour, both sisters left, searching for some dinner. They wandered along and eventually came upon Hope House.

"That's the place I was telling you about." Elka pointed to the building. "They provide emergency shelter to kids who are on the street. Do you mind if I stop in quick and say hello?"

"Not at all. I'll wait right here." Colleen took a seat on the stoop.

Once again, Elka stood at the front door to Hope House, wondering whether to knock or walk inside. She rapped on the door, and Father Bryan answered.

He gave her a warm smile. "Elka, how are you? Good to see you."

She was impressed that he remembered her name. After all, he was meeting new people all the time. "Hi, Father Bryan. I was in the neighborhood, and I just wanted to say hello." She paused. "Well, actually, I also wanted to let you know how Olivia is doing, and once again, say thank you for helping her."

"And how is Olivia?" Father Bryan shut the door behind him and sat down on the front stoop near Colleen. He nodded a greeting to her.

"Oh, sorry. Let me introduce you. Father Bryan, this is my sister, Colleen. Colleen, Father Bryan." After her sister and Father Bryan shook hands, Elka felt comfortable continuing. "I got a letter from Olivia yesterday. She's with a foster family that she seems to like."

"Ah, that's great. I'm glad to hear it. So many times, kids leave this place, and we never get to know about the next chapter in their story." Father Bryan pulled out a pack of gum and held it out toward Elka and Colleen.

Elka took a piece of gum and unwrapped it. "I'm interested in helping out here if there's anything I can do."

"If you're serious, we need someone like you who could serve as sort of a resident advisor for the girls. It doesn't pay much, but room and board are included."

Elka hadn't been asking, specifically, about a full-time job, but now that Father Bryan had brought it up, the idea was appealing. "Wow, that's something I'd like to consider. When would the job start?"

"We need someone right away, but if you need a few weeks to wrap up whatever you're currently doing, that would be fine too." Father Bryan stood. "It's a year-long commitment. Take a few days to think it over, then get back to me."

Elka and Colleen said goodbye, and Elka promised to call Father Bryan in a couple of days. She was quiet on the way back to midtown—lost in her thoughts—and grateful that Colleen was absorbed in a book she'd brought along

There was a lot to consider. New York, Seattle, Jacob, a job she really wanted. It wasn't possible to have it all. She had some big decisions to make. Maybe it would be smart to pray about what to do.

Elka turned to her sister. "Do you want to get up early tomorrow and go to mass with me in the morning?"

CHAPTER TWENTY-FIVE

Jacob reached over and held Elka's hand as the plane began to taxi down the runway. She was perfectly calm, as if hurtling through the sky in a tin can at ten thousand feet was no big deal. Of course. As a model, Elka had traveled extensively. He made an effort to relax his grip and appear more relaxed than he felt.

Just in case, Jacob checked to make sure there was an airsickness bag in the seat pocket. It would be embarrassing if he had to use it, but even worse if there wasn't one available when needed. He felt the plane accelerate, and then, liftoff.

When the plane finally leveled off from the ascent, Jacob opened his eyes and let out the breath he'd been holding. Elka had surely noticed his reaction, but she pretended not to. She opened the book she'd brought along and began reading. It was just another reason he loved her.

Soon the cabin began to fill with cigarette smoke as passengers started to light up. Jacob, who was not a smoker, felt his throat getting scratchy. In an attempt to shift his focus away from the annoyances, he opened the menu to see what was for lunch—shrimp cocktail, filet mignon, baked potato, viscount salad, rolls, and pie. He felt better already, just thinking about it.

When the stewardess came by and offered champagne, both Elka and Jacob accepted. Elka held her glass up. "Here's to the have-beens, the are-nows, and the may-be's."

"Cheers." Jacob clinked her glass and took a drink. The fizzy liquid tickled his tongue. Their future was a big *may-be*, and he wanted to change that. His desire was for Elka to arrive in Seattle, love it, and decide to stay. His hometown might not be as sophisticated or exciting as New York, but August in Seattle was pretty spectacular in its own way.

"There's something I need to tell you." Elka seemed hesitant to continue. "I was offered a position at Hope House a few days ago."

The airplane lurched, and Jacob spilled champagne on himself. Elka offered him a napkin. Jacob took it and dabbed at his shirt. "Oh, really? Are you going to take it?"

"I haven't decided yet. I'll be honest with you. I think I would really enjoy the work. It's the kind of thing I've wanted to do for a while now. But I promise I'm coming to Seattle with an open mind."

"That's all I ask." Jacob tried to keep the tone of his voice upbeat. He didn't want to be pushy. It was Elka's decision to make. If she decided to stay in New York, the distance would be challenging, but they could make it work. He could probably go back to working at the Biltmore each summer. Law school was only for three years, and then they could get married. Who was he kidding? That was a long time. The idea of it was depressing.

Elka turned her attention toward the view outside the window—nothing but big puffy white clouds. What was she thinking about? Did she want him to speak up and let her know how much he wanted her to stay in Seattle? Or was it better to remain quiet and give her some space? Jacob picked up a magazine and started flipping through the pages.

A moment later, a woman's panicked scream startled Jacob from his reading. He spilled the rest of his champagne as the plane veered sharply to the left. Loud shouts came from several people near the cockpit. Elka grabbed onto his arm. Her eyes, wide as saucers, spoke to a fear that matched his own.

A glance toward the source of the commotion told Jacob everything he needed to know. A man was standing in the aisle only a few feet in front of their row. He was young, clean-shaven, and dressed like an ordinary businessman. The only imposing thing about him was that he had a gun pointed at people.

"Nobody moves, or I'll shoot," he said in a menacing tone as the plane leveled back to a horizontal position.

"This is your captain speaking," a voice said over the speakers. "An armed man entered the cockpit a few minutes ago, and I am no longer in control of this flight's direction. Please do not panic. We are going to Chicago, where we will make an emergency landing and where you will be allowed to disembark." The pilot sounded professional. Unruffled.

Then it was eerily quiet, except for the hum of the plane's engine. Jacob took Elka's hand in his own and silently prayed—nothing more than the word, *help*. Elka's knees were shaking, but the rest of her body remained still. The couple across the aisle huddled together with their heads down. Jacob kept his down too. He didn't want to do anything that might call attention. He froze when a pair of large black boots stopped right in front of him. *Please, God, please, let us all live.*

Eventually, the boots continued down the aisle toward the back of the plane. Jacob heard Elka let out a sigh of relief. He watched as she carefully reached into her purse, which was next to her on the seat, and took out a rosary.

She looked at Jacob and mouthed the words, *I love you. It's going to be okay. Pray.*

Jacob nodded and whispered, "I love you too."

A baby started crying. Outside the window, another plane was flying close alongside them— an escort. Jacob and Elka stayed as they were, in their tucked positions, heads down. His muscles were screaming to move.

After what felt like an eternity, though it probably was only a couple of hours, the captain made another announcement over the loud- speaker. "We have enough fuel to make it to Chicago, folks. When we land, please use the emergency exits, and when you are off, immedi- ately, run away from the plane." Emphatic, but once again, professional.

So far, none of the passengers had panicked. At least, not that Jacob was aware of. He credited the flight crew for this. Until the announcement, Jacob hadn't even thought about the possibility of running out of fuel. It was a chilling thought. The man with the gun never said anything else after his initial instruction not to move. He stalked the aisle menacingly, making everyone aware of his presence. Nobody tested him on his threat.

The landing was bumpy, but when the wheels touched down and when the plane stopped, there was a collective sense of cautious relief. Freedom from this nightmare might be within their grasp.

"Go! Go! Go!" someone shouted.

People were pushing open the emergency exits. Jacob saw the slide inflate. There was no time to hesitate. What if the hijackers changed their minds and didn't let them go? He grabbed Elka's hand, and they moved toward the doors. When it was their turn, they jumped together. As soon as their feet hit the ground, they both ran away from the plane, never stopping to look back.

There were multiple ambulances and police cars parked all around the tarmac. One thought repeated itself in Jacob's mind. Stay with Elka. The chaotic activity outside felt jarring after the last few hours of silence and fear. Were they safe yet? Where was the gunman? How many hijackers were there? Was anyone hurt?

"Come with me." Jacob turned to see a man in the driver's seat of a golf cart, waving him and

Elka over for a ride. They accepted his help and took the two empty seats. He took them to an airport hangar that appeared to be a gathering spot for the passengers.

Red Cross volunteers were handing out water and writing people's names down on clipboards. Someone offered Jacob and Elka sandwiches. Elka, who hadn't spoken out loud yet, said a quiet *thank you* and took both sandwiches for them.

"We're going to be all right," Jacob said, working his vocal cords again. It was as if, in speaking the words, it was finally real.

It wasn't until Jacob and Elka started talking to the other people around them that Jacob was finally able to piece together what happened. There were three hijackers. When one of the stewardesses went to deliver lunch to the pilots, two gunmen forced their way into the cockpit. The other one stayed in the cabin. They demanded the pilots take them to Chicago to let the passengers off in exchange for a ransom and fuel for the plane. The pilots were still hostages on the plane, and the rumor was that they would be forced to take the hijackers to Cuba. As far as Jacob could tell, there had been no casualties.

A long queue of traumatized passengers stood waiting to use the phones. Jacob put his arm around Elka. "We need to get in line and call our families ... let them know we're okay."

CHAPTER TWENTY-SIX

Elka felt a dull ache at her temples. After the last thirty hours, all she wanted was to be asleep in her bed at home, not thousands of miles away in a strange city she'd never been before, meeting her boyfriend's family for the first time. But where was home, anyway? Was home her single room at Morgan Hall in midtown Manhattan? Or was it with her family in Danbury, Connecticut?

Dysfunctional as her family was, after thinking she might never see them again, talking to them over the phone last night had been strangely cathartic. The emotion in her parent's voices had been unmistakable, and it told her what she needed to know. They'd been worried about her. News of the hijacking had already reached them by the time she'd called. They did care about her, and Elka loved them, despite everything that had happened in the past. Sure, there was still a lot of forgiveness to work through, but they were her family.

Maybe her home was supposed to be with the lost girls at Hope House. Elka thought about the story of Jonah that she'd heard as a little girl in Sunday School. Jonah was going to the wrong city, so God sent a whale to swallow him and take him where he was supposed to go. Was the plane hijacking a sign from God? Was this her whale? She'd prayed and asked God what to do, but she hadn't heard an answer yet. Maybe she wasn't supposed to be going to Seattle. Perhaps this was God's way of telling her he wanted her to go to West Village.

Of course, she could be way off. Jacob was everything she had ever wanted in a man. Smart, kind, funny, and far too handsome for his own good. He brought out the best in her. And Elka was most content when she was with Jacob. Not to mention, he was calm in a crisis. She'd drawn on his strength yesterday when she'd been more scared than she'd ever been in her life. When it came to Jacob, her heart was all in. But did he feel the same way about her? Did he want to spend a lifetime with her? Was her home supposed to be with him? There were still so many unanswered questions.

The plane was approaching Seattle, and the captain was announcing where passengers could pick up their luggage. She let out a wry laugh. Jacob's and her luggage were probably somewhere in Cuba right about now. Would she ever see her belongings again?

The question felt shameful because they still didn't know what had become of the two pilots. Were they okay? She shivered as images of the black-booted man with a gun entered her thoughts.

"Are you ready?" Jacob's voice brought Elka back to the present.

She was safe, and soon, she would be off this plane. It hadn't been easy, getting on another airplane so quickly, but she and Jacob had both agreed that it was necessary. Elka had a suspicion that if she let fear get the better of her, and if she didn't get on this flight to Seattle, she might never find the courage to fly again.

"We made it." Elka gave Jacob a light kiss on his lips. After everything they'd just been through, they would always share a bond, no matter what happened with their future. "I'm ready."

Elka woke up the next morning feeling well-rested. The three-hour time difference was in her favor. It was like she'd slept late, even though the clock on the bedside table said it was only six. Was anyone else even awake yet? The house was quiet. The luxurious four-poster canopy bed made her feel like a princess. She was content to luxuriate in this peaceful space before the day began.

Last night, Elka was so tired, she'd barely been able to stand upright, and she'd hardly even noticed her surroundings. Now, she took in the guest room, admiring all the lovely details, from the delicate floral wallpaper, the carved mahogany mantle over the fireplace, to the Tiffany wall sconces. Jacob had never mentioned that he'd grown up in such a beautiful home.

Ann and Paul—as they insisted she call them—had been waiting for them at the arrival gate in Seattle. Elka's apprehension over staying with Jacob's parents dissolved after both of them so warmly embraced her. For much of the car ride home, Paul lightened the mood with a steady stream of funny anecdotes about his grandkids, and Ann's tenderness was a comfort to Elka. Jacob's mother had asked just enough questions to indicate she cared, acknowledging the horror of the hijacking, but she'd refrained from pressing either of them for details. She seemed to understand that neither of them was ready to talk about it yet.

Jacob's parents, as excited as they were to see their son, both understood the reality that Elka and Jacob were exhausted after everything they'd just been through. Soon after they'd entered the house, Ann had shown Elka to the guest room. She asked if Elka was hungry, then told her she was looking forward to getting to know her better in the morning after she'd had a good night's rest. It had been the sweetest relief to be released from any sort of expectations to socialize. All Elka had wanted was some food, a hot shower, some solitude, and a soft pillow to lay her head down.

Jacob's mother had already thought of everything Elka might need. Anticipating that Elka wouldn't have any luggage, Ann had given her a nightgown, toothbrush, and a clean set of clean clothes for the morning. *We can go downtown tomorrow and get whatever else you might need.* Ann's kindness was touching, and Elka's nerves were so frayed that embarrassingly, she'd started crying. Ann offered a tissue and a reassuring, motherly hug. Elka recalled Ann's next words. *It's okay, sweetie. You've been through a lot, but you're safe now. We're so happy to have you here. I'll send something up for you to eat. Do you like macaroni and cheese?*

Mac n' cheese was Elka's favorite. A few minutes later, Jacob had knocked on the door, offering a tray with a bowl of the most delicious, creamy macaroni Elka had ever tasted. He kissed her goodnight, then left her to have some time to herself. Now that she'd met his mother a second time, she had a better idea of where he'd learned to be so thoughtful.

The morning light splashed through the lace curtains, and Elka could hear someone moving around downstairs, so she pushed the blankets off and got out of bed, padding over to the chair where Ann had set out a pair of soft gray capris and a white button-up blouse for her to wear—just her size. Elka quickly dressed, put her hair in a ponytail, and then brushed her teeth in the bathroom across the hall.

From what Elka had seen so far, the house was a large, lovely old Victorian. Elka went downstairs, following the voices of Jacob and his mother. She found them sitting together at a small table in the kitchen, drinking coffee and sharing a newspaper.

Ann laid the publication down and stood. "Good morning!" she said, greeting Elka in a chipper voice. "Did you sleep well?"

"I did. Thank you. Your home is so lovely." Elka glanced around the cozy kitchen. Muffins were set out on the countertop, next to a plate with bacon. Her stomach growled.

"Would you like some coffee?" Jacob got up and pulled a mug from the cupboard. He didn't wait for an answer. While pouring her drink, he used his other hand to wave toward the newspaper. "There's some good news in there. Both of the pilots made it home safely. The hijackers thought Castro was going to give them a free pass into his country, but instead, they were arrested as soon as they landed in Cuba."

Elka's mouth fell open with surprise and delight. It was the best possible outcome and not at all what she had been expecting. "Wow, that's fantastic!" Elka smiled as she accepted the coffee from Jacob. She took an empty chair at the table and pulled the newspaper over to see the good news for herself. A photo of the two pilots was included on the front page. True heroes.

Ann brought a plate of food to Elka and set it in front of her. "I'm glad the clothes fit. I wasn't sure. They belong to my daughter, Claire. Are you two up for a big family dinner tonight?" Ann glanced toward Jacob, raising an eyebrow.

"I am. I can't wait to see everyone." Jacob slathered a thick slice of butter on his muffin.

Ann nodded. "I'm excited to meet everyone too." Jacob had already told her many stories about his sisters. She already knew she was going to love them.

"Perfect. Let's plan on seven, okay? By the way ..." Ann put her hand on her son's shoulder. "The airline called. You and Elka can go back to

Sea-Tac and get your luggage today. It's waiting for you."

Elka took a sip of coffee and said a silent prayer of gratitude to God. This morning was off to a great start. It almost felt too good to be true. Was it?

After breakfast, Elka followed Jacob into the front sitting room. A large picture window offered a view of the city that was truly spectacular, like a postcard. The house was situated at the top of a hill. She could see what she already knew was Elliot Bay, with little boats bobbing about, and beyond that was Mt. Rainier, like a giant marshmallow poking through the clouds. Prominently featured in the middle of this scene was a tower with a flying saucer at the top—the Space Needle.

Jacob sat on a bench in front of a grand piano and began tinkering with the keys. Elka joined him. "Do you play?"

Jacob shrugged a shoulder and gave a sheepish smile. "A little. I've missed having a piano."

A collection of framed family photos sat on the piano lid. Elka studied each one, thinking how they seemed like such a happy family. One silver frame caught Elka's attention. Instead of a picture, it had a scripture verse, written in calligraphy on creamy white paper.

For we are God's handiwork, created in Christ Jesus to do good works, which God prepared in advance for us to do. ~ Ephesians 2:10

Was the job at Hope House the good work God had prepared for her? And what if she chose to move to Seattle instead?

CHAPTER TWENTY-SEVEN

Claire, Troy, and the five-year-old twins, Michelle and Maria, arrived first. They were gathered at the base of the staircase in the front entry. "I suppose you'll be wanting these back." Claire dangled a set of keys in front of Jacob. When he reached to take them from his sister, she swiped them away teasingly. "Or maybe, I'll keep it. I've grown pretty attached to Little Red."

"You named my car?" He grinned, then poked his head out the front door, confirming that his Mustang really was parked out front. Then he pulled Claire into a bear hug while taking the keys from her at the same time. He couldn't wait to get behind the wheel, take Elka for a spin, and show her the city.

While Jacob was introducing Elka to his sister and her family, his other sister, MaryAnne, and her family arrived. She and her husband, Michael, had a four-year-old son named Billy. Like a switch suddenly flipped, the house's atmosphere changed from quiet and calm to the more familiar, boisterous ruckus that Jacob had grown up with. It was just the way he liked it.

By the time dinner was over, later that night, Elka had been initiated into the ways of the Lewis clan. Jacob had worried, unnecessarily, that his family might overwhelm her when they were all together. They were a noisy bunch, but they were always a lot of fun. Jacob was proud of Elka and beyond pleased to see how his family got along with her. He loved the way her dark eyes sparkled when she laughed, and she'd laughed a lot tonight.

When the house was still again, and it was well past eleven, Jacob walked up the stairs with Elka and paused in front of her door. "Did you have fun tonight?"

"Yes! I love your family. Billy, Michelle, and Maria are adorable." Her eyes darted about the hallway. Then she touched his lips with a slow, sweet kiss. Jacob didn't want it to end.

Jacob heard footsteps coming up the stairs. He backed away from Elka, though he didn't want to. "Goodnight. I'll see you in the morning."

Settled in his old bedroom, Jacob tried to sleep, but he lay awake for a long time. His mother had left everything just as it was when he'd moved out four years ago. Old football trophies still lined the shelves, a poster from the 1962 Seattle World's Fair hung on the wall, and his guitar was propped up against the wall in the corner. The room hadn't changed, but he had.

Tomorrow he'd take Elka to Ivar's to get fish and chips for lunch, and after that, maybe they'd visit the observation deck at the Space Needle. Too bad he couldn't treat her to dinner there. Unfortunately, his bank account needed some replenishment. A meal at the Space Needle would have to wait until next time and so would a marriage proposal. He needed an engagement ring, and only the best would do.

Jacob glanced over at Elka in the passenger seat. They were cruising along Interstate 5, heading toward the airport. The wind whipped at the emerald-colored silk scarf she'd tied over her hair. A pair of dark sunglasses covered most of her face. He couldn't read her expression. She'd been quiet for most of the last thirty minutes. Was it a contented silence? Or was she feeling the same kind of pain that was ripping at his heart right now? The lump in Jacob's throat grew more prominent the closer they got to their destination. He didn't want to say goodbye.

Their time together had gone too fast, and Jacob was feeling a pang of regret over buying a round-trip ticket for Elka. Not that he wasn't glad she'd come out to Seattle. Jacob just wished she didn't have to go back to New York. Of course, the whole idea of this visit had been to avoid pressuring her to relocate, and he still didn't want to do that. So he swallowed the question he wanted to ask. It was up to Elka, and she would let him know when she was ready.

The whole time Elka had been here, it had been sunny and in the seventies. She'd seen Seattle at its best. Was that really fair? Until now, Jacob had downplayed the nine months of the year when the gray skies and drizzle his city was known for settled in like a thick blanket. The weather didn't bother him, but he should probably let Elka know the full reality of what she might be in for. Maybe that could be something to include in his first letter to her. He was going to have to get used to writing.

They were at the airport now. After parking the Mustang, Jacob opened the trunk to retrieve her suitcase. Elka opened her purse and pulled out her itinerary. She furrowed her brow as she scanned the information. "Let me see, where do I need to go ..."

"You know, you could just throw that away, and we could just turn around and go back." He was only half-kidding.

Elka laughed. "A-7, it says."

Checking the bag and finding her gate provided a temporary distraction, but there was nothing more to do but say goodbye as soon as all that was done. "Will you please call me when you arrive? I want to know you arrived safely."

"Yes ... thank you so much. I had the best time. Your family was so welcoming. I'm sorry I haven't given you an answer yet. I—I need a little more time."

Jacob wrapped her in his arms, inhaling the clean, citrusy scent of her hair. She turned her face toward him, and he kissed her. "Take whatever time you need." He tucked a chestnut-colored strand of hair behind her ear. She was so beautiful, inside and out. "Claire told me to mention that you have a standing offer to take the guest room in her house if you want to come back on a more permanent basis. She would love to have you, and I'm sure she wouldn't mind some extra help with the twins."

"I'll think about it. I promise." A voice over the loudspeaker announced Flight 216, Seattle to New York, was boarding. Elka straightened her shoulders and took a deep breath. "I love you."

"I love you too." Why did it sound like she was saying goodbye to him for good? Was he just reading too much into the situation? Jacob kissed her again, then watched her go. Elka waved one last time before she handed the gate agent her ticket.

Jacob stayed behind to watch Elka's plane take off. His heart ached as it took her away. He wasn't sure when—or if—he would see her again.

CHAPTER TWENTY-EIGHT

Elka walked down the grand staircase into the lobby and paused, taking a moment to appreciate her surroundings. Her shift in the Palm Court started in twenty minutes. She was going to miss this place when it was time to leave. The Biltmore Hotel had been a soft-landing spot after her exit from modeling and the break with her parents. Alone in the city, broke, and seeking a fresh start, she'd come here, found a job, and also some wonderful friends.

Mr. Barrows had taken her under his wing and mentored her. He'd seen her potential, given her opportunities for advancement, and made sure she was provided for when she broke her ankle. And for that, she would always be grateful. Her boss made no secret of the fact that he wanted to see Elka move into a management role and work her way up—a flattering idea. But hotel management wasn't what she wanted to do with her life. Her time here had been a respite and a way to earn an income. Now it was time to move on.

She might find Mr. Barrows in the lobby. Elka needed to give him her notice. It would be hard to disappoint him, but it was time to have this conversation. Much to her surprise, instead of Mr. Barrows, she found her family. All three of them were standing near the concierge desk. What were they doing here?

A quick phone conversation last night had updated her sister on Elka's return. Colleen told her the hijacking had shaken their parents, but she hadn't mentioned coming into the city with them today.

Elka rushed over to greet them. Her mother dropped the bag she was holding, and quite un-characteristically, pulled Elka into an embrace. When she let go and stepped back, her mother had tears in her eyes. Elka glanced at her father, who'd shoved his hands into his pockets. He shrugged and cleared his throat. Colleen stood a few feet away, barely containing an amused smirk.

"We're staying here tonight and just checked in," her father said. "We decided it was time to visit you. Colleen said you were working today, but perhaps when you're done, we could go get dinner?" His voice held a hint of warmth.

"I—I'm done at five. Dinner would be nice." Elka was nearly speechless. "Thank you. It's—it's nice to see you."

Elka's mother, who'd now recovered from her momentary burst of emotion, busied herself with taking off her gloves, one finger at a time. "We're just glad you made it back in one piece. "Meet us in the lobby tonight at six?"

"Yes. Okay." Elka glanced at the clock across the lobby. She was out of time.

"Well then, we'll let you go now." Her mother gave her an air kiss. "See you later."

Her father gave Elka a nod and followed his wife toward the elevators. Her sister was now applying a coat of pink lip gloss. She smooshed her lips together and tossed the tube in her purse. Colleen still hadn't said anything.

Elka furrowed her brows and mouthed the words, *Why didn't you tell me?*

Colleen smiled, whispered a quick, "Sorry," then turned on her heel and followed her parents.

Elka's intense curiosity made the following six hours of work feel more like twelve. She reminded herself to keep her expectations low. She had long ago given up on hoping for any apology from her father. *People don't change overnight*. She'd been on her own in the city for three years now. Her parents hadn't ever come to have dinner with her. What did their presence here mean?

A table of six ladies stayed long past closing time, laughing and visiting with each other. When, at last, they finally left, Elka only had a few minutes to rush upstairs to the locker room to take off her uniform and freshen her appearance. She put on the sleeveless pink shift she'd been wearing earlier. It wasn't proper dinner attire, but it would have to do. There wasn't enough time to run home and change.

Elka's family was waiting for her in the lobby when she went back down. Her father told them he'd made reservations at Vittorio's down the street. Elka nodded with approval. The restaurant was her favorite place for spaghetti. It was everything one might expect from a place called Vittorio's—red-checkered tablecloths, mustachioed waiters who spoke with Italian accents, a band that played Dean Martin covers, and one very passionate chef.

"What did you all do this afternoon?" Elka asked as they walked out the front doors of the Biltmore. She kept her voice light. They must be feeling the same awkwardness hanging in the air. It was as if all the things left unsaid over the years had stacked up, creating a wall that was nearly impossible to scale.

Colleen cleared her throat. "We went to the Met. They have a new exhibit on fashion through the eighteenth century. There were some beautiful gowns there."

The trip to the art museum provided something to talk about for the next few minutes. Once they were seated at the restaurant, a waiter brought over menus and a basket of delicious, warm bread.

"We'd like to hear about your trip to Seattle." Elka's mother closed her menu. "And tell us about Jacob. How did you two meet?"

Elka wasn't sure where to begin. "I met Jacob at work ..." She went on to tell them about how he'd helped her over the summer—first with getting around the city on crutches, and then, with the search for Olivia, and finally, how he was now starting law school in his hometown. The more she shared, the more she realized what a fantastic person he was, how supportive he'd been, and how much she already missed him.

She finished by saying, "Seattle is a beautiful place. I think you would all like it. It's very clean, and it's surrounded by water and mountains."

Colleen took a sip of water, then she set the glass down and took a deep breath. She narrowed her eyes and gave Elka her full attention. "I can't believe I'm saying this ... but why don't you find a job in Seattle so you can be with Jacob? What's keeping you here?"

We're not even engaged. But Elka kept that thought to herself. "I—I was just offered a job at Hope House. I'll be helping kids like Olivia. It's something I think I could be good at, and it feels like important work."

Elka's father shook his head. "You don't think there are kids like Olivia in Seattle?"

At that moment, the waiter came to take their order. Elka was grateful for the distraction. Colleen's suggestion had been unexpected. And her father, who rarely spoke to her, had just said something that sounded an awful lot like fatherly advice. It was a lot to take in.

The waiter left, and Elka's mother focused her attention on her daughter. "Elka, you've always been someone who takes care of other people. And you're right, that's important work. But sometimes I wonder if you realize that your happiness is also important. Where would you be happiest? Seattle or New York?"

Elka took another piece of bread and slathered butter over it. "It's complicated, but I appreciate what you said. I'm still thinking, but I'm going to Hope House tomorrow, after work. I'll need to give Father Bryan an answer."

Later that night, after Elka said goodbye to her family, she crawled into bed with a smile on her face. She felt lighter, despite all the pasta she'd consumed. Her parents were trying, in their own way, to make things right with her. It was enough.

On Saturday morning, Jacob woke up early. He planned to mow his parents' lawn and catch up on some school reading. His sisters and their families were all coming over for dinner that evening, and he didn't want the weight of unfinished homework hanging over his head when they arrived.

It was Jacob's first day off in a week. He'd started his new job in the dining room at the Broadmoor Golf Club and his classes at Seattle University. The schedule was going to be busy, which was just fine by him. Less time to think about how much he already missed Elka.

Elka was probably moving into her new digs at Hope House today. The last time they'd spoken on the phone, nearly a week ago, she told him she'd put in her notice at the Biltmore. Jacob still had some apprehension about his girlfriend living in the same neighborhood where he'd been robbed at knifepoint. It wasn't the safest place to hang out, but Jacob knew that worrying wouldn't help. Instead, he was getting in the habit of praying more often.

A chill hung in the air that morning. Fall was on its way. Jacob threw on a pair of jeans and his old Columbia sweatshirt, then went down to the kitchen to get some coffee. His father was standing at the stove, making pancakes.

"Morning," Jacob said. He took a mug out of the cupboard.

"Good morning. Want some bacon with your pancakes?"

"Sure. Thank you." Living with his parents again had its perks. "Hey, do you know if there's gas in the lawnmower? I was going to cut the grass this morning."

"Yes, it should be good to go. Appreciate that. I'm going to pick up some steaks later for dinner tonight. Thought I'd fire up the grill one more time before it gets too cold. It should still be warm enough to eat on the back patio, right?"

"Yeah, I think so. Do you want me to set up some tables out there?"

"That would be helpful. We'll have twelve tonight, including the kids. Claire said she was bringing an extra person along."

"Sure thing." Jacob filled a plate with pancakes and took them to the table.

After breakfast, he got to work in the yard. After four years of living in Manhattan, having some grass to mow felt like a wonderful novelty. When he was done with the lawn, Jacob took his books to the hammock strung between two trees in the back part of the property and settled in for some reading. Except for some birds chirping, it was a quiet place to study.

Jacob's mother brought him a ham sandwich and a Coke at lunchtime. He was definitely getting spoiled. *No complaints here.* His mother was humming and practically dancing as she moved around. She was always a cheerful person, but something had her in an especially good mood today.

At some point, Jacob must have fallen asleep in the hammock, and he lost track of time. The sound of children startled him awake.

"Uncle Jacob, we have a surprise for you!"

The twins, Michelle and Maria, came running toward him. Jacob felt a thwack as they both jumped into the hammock with him. All three of them were promptly dumped onto the ground as the sudden motion tipped it upside down.

They were laughing when Jacob noticed a pair of white Keds with red shoelaces come near. His heart skipped a beat. It couldn't be ... He looked up, then blinked, and did a double-take. "Are you my surprise?" Jacob jumped to his feet and swooped Elka into an embrace. "Wh-what are you doing here?"

She laughed. "I live here now. Your family invited me to the cookout." Elka gave a wink to the girls. They were jumping up and down, obviously delighted to be in on the fun. "Is that a good surprise?"

"The best ever." Jacob didn't care who was watching. He leaned down and kissed Elka.

CHAPTER TWENTY-NINE

Claire and Troy's house was located on a hill three and a half blocks from the nearest bus stop. Elka's leg muscles burned as she hurriedly walked home through the rain. Dusk was already setting in, and her shoes were soaked through. She'd only been here a week, but it was already apparent, she needed to learn how to drive. Soon.

Elka had just spent the better part of a day taking the bus to and from Renton, a suburb north of Seattle. It was where the nearest Hope House was located. Seattle had many redeeming qualities, but the public transportation system wasn't one of them. A trip that should have taken only fifteen minutes had taken more than an hour each way.

The long commute had been worth it, though, and nothing was going to spoil Elka's good mood. Thanks to a glowing recommendation from Father Bryan, her interview had gone well. She was the new assistant director for Hope House in Renton. What, exactly, this entailed wasn't entirely clear yet, but Elka couldn't wait to tell Jacob. He was picking her up in less than thirty minutes. This wasn't much time to get ready, considering the current drowned rat look she had going. All she knew was that they were going out to dinner, and he'd hinted that she might want to dress up.

Jacob's red Mustang was already parked on the street in front of his sister's house when Elka arrived. He was early.

When Elka walked in the front door, Michelle and Maria excitedly greeted her. "Can we come with you and Uncle Jacob tonight?" Maria asked.

Michelle did a little pirouette. She wore her ballet slippers, as usual. "Where are you going?"

Ruby, the family's golden retriever, licked Elka's hand. She loved the happy chaos that was a part of living in this household. Elka hugged each of the girls and gave Ruby a scratch on the head. "I don't know where we're going ..."

"No little munchkins tagging along tonight, girls." Jacob appeared in the foyer, wearing a suit and looking so handsome, he could have passed for a movie star.

Elka gave Jacob a quick kiss on the cheek. "Let me just run upstairs and change real quick."

Ten minutes later, Elka was ready to go, wearing a simple black A-line dress, pearls, and high heels. She'd pulled her hair into a bun and applied some red lipstick. "I'm ready!" she called out as she bounded down the stairs.

Jacob was waiting at the bottom of the stairs. He raised his eyebrows and cleared his throat. "You are gorgeous. Let's go."

He was always complimenting her like that. Elka loved the way he made her feel. She smiled. "Thank you."

Jacob opened the front door. "Bye, Claire. Bye, girls."

When he pulled the car up to the base of the Space Needle, five minutes later, Elka realized this was no ordinary date night. A valet opened the door and helped her out of the Mustang. She waited for Jacob to come around the side of the car. Then he took her hand and led her inside.

Elka felt a little breathless as she got into the elevator. It ran up the building's side, and all but the interior door was made of glass. She took in the fantastic view as they quickly rose far above the city. She'd been here with Jacob once before, but only to the observation deck.

This time they were going to Sky City, the revolving restaurant at the top. But it wasn't the scenery, nor was it the anticipation of a good meal that had Elka's heart racing. It was the gut feeling she had about why Jacob had brought her here. He was acting similarly to the time he'd taken her to the Rainbow Room and given her the ticket to Seattle—nervous. Instinct told her she was standing on the precipice of something significant.

The door of the elevator opened onto a foyer, and a hostess greeted them. She led them to a table and handed them their menus. They both decided they wanted to try the "Jet Set Special," which was fondue for two.

"How'd your interview go today?" Jacob asked.

"You're looking at the new Assistant Director of Hope House in Renton." Elka grinned.

"Oh, wow ... that's great!"

Elka knew Jacob was sincere, and she loved that about him. He was genuinely supportive of her goals.

Over the next hour, Elka relaxed and enjoyed the meal, along with the unique experience of watching the view outside change as the building slowly rotated. People set birthday cards on the window ledge next to the table. Since the floor rotated, the cards moved along from table to table, allowing other diners to add messages of goodwill as they went by. Throughout the dinner, Elka and Jacob wrote their best wishes and names on a couple of cards. It was a fun way to honor a stranger's important day.

Sky City was a special occasion restaurant, and Elka was anxious to get to the reason why they were there. Since it wasn't her birthday, something else was going on. Jacob was probably waiting until dessert to reveal what he had in mind.

After the waiter brought out some chocolate cake and coffee and left, Elka knew she was right. Jacob reached into the inside of his jacket and pulled out a small velvet box. He got out of his chair and kneeled in front of her on one knee, holding out the box. She opened it and gasped with delight at the beautiful art deco diamond ring. Overjoyed and overwhelmed, her heart felt like it was flipping inside her chest.

"I love you, Elka," Jacob said, his voice cracking with emotion. "I want to spend the rest of my life with you. Will you marry me?"

Elka wiped away a joyful tear. Her life was about to change, and she felt confident in her answer. "Yes ... I love you too."

<u>E P I L O G U E</u>

June 1969

"**I** have the keys. How about I drive today?" Elka called out to Jacob. She peered out the kitchen window toward the driveway where the car was parked.

"Okay, I'll just let Wanda know we're leaving. Then, we're ready."

Wanda was one of the counselors who volunteered at Hope House. She was in charge when Elka and Jacob weren't home. There were only four young women in residence right now, but as house parents, Jacob and Elka's job was to make sure there was always a staff member at the house. They needed to be prepared to welcome any young woman in crisis, and they never knew when one might show up.

Elka jiggled the keys in her hand as she waited. She could barely contain her excitement. The last time she'd seen her sister was at the wedding, during Christmas. They had a lot to catch up on. Colleen was done with her sophomore year at Barnard and would be spending the next couple of months in Seattle. Jacob's law classes were continuing through the summer, which would keep him busy. Elka was looking forward to having her sister's company—and her help. Hope House was a sprawling two-story home that needed constant maintenance. Elka planned to put Colleen to work, painting the main living areas and cleaning up the yard's overgrown landscaping.

"Should we put the top down?" Elka asked as they walked out of the house. It was a beautiful day.

"Sounds good to me. Are you sure you want to drive? The traffic is going to be pretty bad this time of day."

"I'm sure." Elka opened the driver's side door. When Jacob got in on the passenger side, she leaned over and kissed her husband. It would be fun to see Colleen's expression when she pulled up to the curb at Sea-Tac airport behind the wheel of the Mustang. "Colleen doesn't know I learned how to drive. I want to surprise her."

Jacob smiled. "I know you've missed her. Do you still think moving to Seattle was a good idea? Are you happy here?"

"Best decision ever. I'm happy being wherever you are."

Acknowledgments

I want to send a big thank you to my wonderful editor. You have taught me so much, and I appreciate your patience and kind encouragement. You make me a better writer.

Grace, my first beta reader, thank you! Amanda and Jessica, my critique partners, you're the best!

My family: I couldn't do this without your love and support.

***

I sincerely hope you enjoyed reading Biltmore Girl. I love writing and sharing stories that entertain and inspire curiosity about historical events.

Please know, reviews help authors, and I appreciate and read them! It would mean so much to me if you left a review. You can do that here.

***

The Historic Hotels Collection

Seattle
1938

Chicago
1892

New York
1968

Ann + Paul

Elizabeth + John

Elka + Jacob

www.dawnklinge.com

Dawn Klinge is a Pacific Northwest native who loves a rainy day, a hot cup of coffee, and a good book to get lost in. This wife and mom to two young adults is often inspired by true personal and historical accounts. Dawn is a member of the American Christian Fiction Writers Association. Her other books in the Historic Hotels Collection are Sorrento Girl and Palmer Girl.

www.dawnklinge.com